Love of a Lifetime

I0680549

By: Denise Hill

Acknowledgments

First and foremost, I want to thank God for giving me the determination, wisdom and courage to see this project through. I also want to thank my son Daniel and my daughter Devin and friends for their encouragement and support. Special thanks go out to Lolita Smith for her editing and advice, DH Publishing and Heather Gum for the cover design and Aurora Production for their photography. Last, but not least, I want to thank Dwight Cliff for being Jordan.

DH Publishing Co

Indianapolis, IN 46229

Love of a Lifetime

Cover design: DH Publishing Co

ISBN: 978-0615687643

0615687644

Prologue

Jordan steps out of the shower just as Jasmine walks in. She stands there in awe as she eyes the man that has hunted her dreams for years. Jasmine allows the towel that covers her naked body to drop to the floor, exposing herself to him. Within seconds, the two bodies collide. Jasmine runs her hand over Jordan's defined chest and feels the rapid beating of his heart. Jordan drops his head pressing his lips to the nape of her neck noticing a shudder from her. He cradles her face between his palms kissing her mouth the column of her neck then to the base of her throat. When he returns to her lips, their tongues meet in a slow sensual dance of desire. Her taste, the smell of her skin holds him captive. He wants to spend hours in her scented embrace, but reality snaps him back as he pulls away and stares at her. "We can't do this Jasmine."

Jordan grabs the towel lying on the bathroom counter and wraps it around his body as he makes his way to his bedroom where he sits in silence wondering what just happened. Jasmine is speechless and the tears began to flow. Her thoughts and feelings were weighing her down. Biting down on her lower lip, she tries to bring her emotions under control, but against her will, she is falling in love with Jordan.

CHAPTER 1

December 31, 2008

New Year's Eve

Jordan sits on the edge of his desk as he phones his wife. He glances over at a picture of her and his baby while thinking back to the day when she gave birth and named her after him, Jordan Denise Daniels. He was so excited. He called everyone he could think of to tell them that he is the father of a healthy seven-pound baby girl; JD is the splitting image of him.

"Hey babe." "How's my little one?"

"I put her down for a nap about twenty minutes ago. She was rather cranky today and continued to spit up. I don't think the milk agrees with her stomach. I called her doctor and he told me to put her on soymilk and see how she does. Mom ran to the store for me and got a container of soymilk. I gave her a bottle before she fell asleep, so far she's doing good."

"Good, and how is my beautiful Queen doing?"

"She's fine; just waiting for her wonderful King to arrive."

Jordan laughs.

"I will be there in no time, I am expecting an important delivery so I am hanging around until it arrives. How are things coming along for the party?"

"It's moving slower than I expected. Mom and I finished decorating and the caterers should be here within a few hours. Tonight is going to be special for us honey. I refused to allow anything or anyone to ruin this for us."

"I know sweetheart. I'll join you in a little while."

"Okay be careful out on the road. I love you Mr. Daniels."

"I love you more Mrs. Daniels."

Jordan hangs around the office waiting on the courier to deliver a package he will present to Jasmine this evening. The surprise is a copy of his first novel he wrote and kept hidden from her until tonight. The two endured so much in the past year that he decided to turn his daily journal into a book. He wants the world to know what he and his wife had gone through in order to get to the point they are today. Sometimes people do not know some of the things one has to face before you end up in a place in life where God wants you.

It has not always peaches and cream for them but they appreciate all of life's experiences because it made them better people and taught them not to take anything or anyone for granted. Jordan realizes now that he had to go through the bad relationships in order for him to be grateful for the good one that came along when he least expected.

Jordan is sitting in his office when the elevator doors open. He steps outside into the hall and walks to the receptionist area to greet the courier.

"Good afternoon sir. I have a delivery for Jordan Daniels."

"I'll take that. You do not know what this means to me," Jordan says as he signs for the package.

The young man hands Jordan the bundle, "Happy New Year," the courier tells Jordan.

"Same to you. Stay safe."

Jordan walks back to his office to open the parcel. The cover brings tears to his eyes. A picture of his wife and his baby is starring back at him. The titled is _Love of a Lifetime_. They are truly a Love of a Lifetime to him. Jordan shuts off his computer, grabs his jacket and heads out.

Forty-five minutes later, Jordan pulls into his driveway. He turns off the engine and sits admiring his home. This is truly a home. Before it was just a house, he thinks to himself. Now he has a loving wife and an adorable child to greet him everyday. Right then, Jordan realizes how blessed he is. He is living the life he has always dreamed of, but he will never forget the ordeal that transpired a year ago. If not for his faith in God and his family standing by him at a time in need, he knows he would not be where he is today.   He also knows if not for his younger brother and his best friend who found Jasmine after her abduction, he would not only lost the love of his life but his daughter would never exist.

NOVEMBER 20, 2007

One year earlier

   Jordan stands staring out of his office window at the black and gray building adjacent to the one he occupies. Jordan admires the modern structure of the building and how the black shimmers as the sun gazes upon it. The building occupies bank employees and attorneys. The building also occupies the corporate office of Cole Laboratory owned by his fiancée Vanessa Cole. This building is where Jordan first laid eyes on the woman he thought to be the woman of his dreams.

   Jordan had been out on appointments this particular morning meeting with several leasing agencies. His company had outgrown its current location. Jordan is looking to relocate. He decides on the downtown area.

   Jordan was on his way to his last appointment. He arrived at the CRA building around 12:15 when he spots a parking spot in front. He quickly maneuvers into the tight space before anyone beats him to it. The only problem Jordan sees with the location is the lack of parking. He hopes the location he chose has affordable parking for his employees. As he enters the building, he forgets what floor the

~ X ~

leasing agency is on. So he decides to check with the guard stationed in the middle of the lobby. Jordan heads toward the guard when he makes eye contact with Vanessa. He is so absorbed in checking her out he had not noticed the man standing in front of him.

"Can I help you sir?" the security guard asks.

"Yes, can you tell me what floor the McFarland Leasing Agency is on?"

"I'm sorry sir, but they are located across the street on the 13th floor."

Feeling like a complete idiot, Jordan turns to leave but not before stealing one last glance at Vanessa. He thinks she is stunning, but he is not the only one who thinks so judging by the blatant male attention she is getting. Vanessa stands at 5'7" with shoulder length hair. Her light brown complexion highlighted with a few brown freckles which catch his attention, but her curvy body is what really captivates Jordan's full attention and attracts him to her. She is wearing a black knit dress with black stilettos. The dress clings to her body outlining a curvy voluptuous body. A body like hers is notorious for driving men crazy.

Jordan had not noticed but he was causing a little attention to himself. Several women in the lobby walk by giving inviting looks and smiles.

Vanessa stands mesmerized by the man standing at the guard's station. It has been a long time since anyone captured her attention like this. He is simply gorgeous. She did not know what, but something about him demanded attention and attention he is getting.

Vanessa recognizes Jordan from an article she read last week on Black Successful Bachelors in Indianapolis. She is impressed to say the least. She thinks like many other women that she would look good on his arm.

Vanessa watches as several women walk by Jordan giving him the eye. Shaking her head she decides she has more to do with her time than to drool over a man. Vanessa pushes the button to the elevator to take her to her office on the executive floor.

Fearing he will make a complete fool of himself, Jordan makes his way across the street to his next appointment where he meets with Donna James the leasing agent for McFarland Leasing Company.

Donna escorts Jordan to the 16th floor. The view alone astounds him. He cannot believe the size. It is 4 times the size of his current location. The space can easily house over 400 employees and the way his company is growing, the space is what he needs.

Jordan walks into the office he will occupy. The room is spacious. He thinks he definitely will need more furniture to fill up the additional space.

Jordan spends about an hour with Donna observing the rest of the floor and going over the leasing contract. Jordan is so impressed and moves his company within four weeks.

After the move, which proved to be good for Jordan's company, he acquired some of the largest accounts from several Fortune 500 companies.

Jordan started JD processing 15 years ago with only 10 employees. Today he employs over 100 people and his company is still growing. With nearly 5,000,000 in revenue and over 650 clients, his company is the fifth largest provider of business outsourcing solutions offering the widest range of payroll, tax and benefits administration solutions from a single source.

Jordan's family suggested he cut his staff because of the continuous loss his company experienced year after year, but he refused to let any of his employees go. Something told him that his company would be successful and he was right.

On occasion when Jordan leaves his office for lunch, he runs into Vanessa several times before asking her out. Their first date started out with dinner at St. Elmo's, a Tyler Perry play and a nightcap at Jordan's lasting until the next morning. Jordan and Vanessa began seeing each other on a regular basis. The two seemed inseparable. Whenever you see Jordan out, Vanessa was right by his side.

Jordan had fallen head over heels in love with Vanessa. He had given her his heart and proposed to her after a short period, but like the others, she broke his heart. Jordan tried so hard to forgive Vanessa for sleeping with his friend and right-hand man. He now realizes he can never forgive any woman who is unfaithful to him.

CHAPTER 2

Jordan turns his attention to the traffic below. He stares at the individuals as they make their way to work, while others wait patiently at the bus stop for their bus to take them to their next destination. He wonders as he watch people laugh and talk with each other, if they are truly happy. Jordan has everything a man could want. He is a successful executive who owns a five-story home, drives a $90,000.00 Mercedes, and to top it off, Jordan is gorgeous. He stands at 6'2" with a muscular build. His complexion is a rich dark Hershey's chocolate which highlights his light- brown eyes. He keeps his head shaved, the conservative look and goatee complements his chiseled features along with the diamond-studded earrings he sports in both ears. Women flock to Jordan. He is one of the hottest and most successful bachelors in Indianapolis. However, with all this, Jordan still experiences a void in his life that no amount of money or success could fulfill.

Jordan wants and needs someone whom he can trust and respect, a person who will love him for him and not for what he has. This is something Jordan longed for but has never experienced in any relationship.

The telephone rings startling Jordan who is so consumed in his thoughts that he shuts out everything around him. It rings again. The flashing of the red light indicates the call is coming through on his private line. Glancing at the clock on the wall, he notices the time and wonders if Ronnie is calling. Jordan had come in early for a 7:30 a.m. meeting with a PI, who happens to be his best friend from college. Jordan finds out someone is embezzling money from his company. Three months ago, Jordan comes across a forged check for $9,500.00 payable to a Tony Carter. To this day, he holds six canceled checks totaling 57,000.00 written to the same person.

Jordan reaches for the receiver on the fifth ring. "Hello, Jordan speaking."

"What took you so long to answer the phone?" Danielle asks. Danielle is Jordan's youngest sibling.

"What's up with the attitude so early this morning?"

"I can't go into that me right now."

Jordan chuckles to himself. His baby sister is nothing more than a drama queen.

"I'm not going to keep you long. I wanted to pass on some good news to you. Are you sitting down?

"No, why?"

"I think you need to sit down for this."

Jordan takes a seat behind his desk. "Okay, I'm seated. Now lay it on me."

"Guess who moved back to town and divorced her husband?"

"Danielle, I know you did not call me this early to play your guessing games. Now tell me who you're talking about." Jordan says with annoyance in his voice.

"Jasmine is back in town and she is no longer married."

Jordan leans back in his chair with the receiver glued to his ear. He sits in deep thought as Danielle rambles on about this and about that. He thinks back to the time Jasmine had come on to him and remembers how devastated she was when he walked away from her.

Jordan steps out of the shower just as Jasmine walks in. She stands there in awe as she eyes the man that has hunted her dreams for years. Jasmine allows the towel that covers her naked body to drop to the floor, exposing herself to him. Within seconds, the two bodies collide. Jasmine runs her hand over Jordan's defined chest and feels the rapid beating of his heart. Jordan drops his head pressing his lips to the nape of her neck noticing a shudder from her. He cradles her face between his palms kissing her mouth the column of her neck then to the base of her throat. When he returns to her lips, their tongues meet in a slow sensual dance of desire. Her taste, the smell of her skin holds him captive. He wants to spend hours in her scented embrace, but reality snaps him back as he pulls away and stares at her. "We can't do this Jasmine."

Jordan grabs the towel lying on the bathroom counter and wraps it around his body as he makes his way to his bedroom where he sits in silence wondering what just happened.

Jasmine is speechless, and he tears began to flow. Her thoughts and feelings were weighing her down. Biting down on her lower lip, she tries to bring her emotions under control, but against her will, she is falling in love with Jordan.

Over the years, Jordan thought a lot about Jasmine. He wondered how things would have turned out for them if she had been a little older. Jordan still remembers the kiss they shared. It was something he doesn't think he will ever forget. He wanted her badly but he did what he believed was right and walked away.

"Jordan are you listening?"

"Yes, I'm here."

"Did you hear anything I said?"

"My hearing is perfect. When did she move back?"

"Mom invited her over for Thanksgiving dinner so you can ask her when you see her. Well I need to run. I will talk to you later, love you."

This was the best news Jordan had heard in months.

After hanging up with Danielle, Jordan sits daydreaming. He is still sitting when Ronnie walks in. Ronnie stands in the doorway. He calls out to Jordan a couple of times before walking over to stand in front of him. Ronnie waves his hand back and forth.

"Hello, is anyone home?"

Jordan jumps startling Ronnie.

"Man are you okay?"

Jordan stands, grinning from ear to ear, as he walks around to the front of his desk to embrace his best friend.

Jordan and Ronnie share a brotherly connection since their college days at Ball State. They are as different as night and day, but they bring a unique balance to their relationship.

"It's good to see you. How's the wife and my girls?"

"They are doing fine. Sheila says to give you her love. Man she cannot wait to see you. Your mom called last week and invited us over for Thanksgiving dinner."

"Oh yeah, I think she did mention something to me about that."

"Jordan, what's up with you?" Ronnie can sense more is going on with Jordan than he lets on. Jordan has always been on top of everything. Now he seems to be preoccupied.

"I'm good, let me to grab my folder. We can use the conference room down the hall."

Ronnie and Jordan sit looking over Jordan's bank statements and canceled checks. Ronnie decides he can no longer keep his thoughts and concerns to himself. "Jordan I can't believe you let this shit go on this long. "What's up with you?"

"After finding the third check, I did some investigating of my own but I came up empty-handed, that's why I called you. Mr. Jones the banking center manager believes it is someone within the company. I cannot believe one of my employees would do this to me. I guess what I am trying to say is that I cannot believe Thomas would do this to me. I didn't think he would stoop this low. It is bad enough he slept with Vanessa, but to steal money from my company. I have been nothing but a good friend to him."

"Hold up, hold up! Are you telling me that Thomas works for you?"

Jordan shakes his head. "He is my accounting manager. I took him under my wing when he was down and out and taught him everything he knows today."

~ XX ~

"Have you lost your mind? I would have fired his ass when I caught him in bed with my girl."

"Don't get me wrong. I wanted to fire him amongst other things, but I really don't have any legal grounds. But if I find out he's behind this, I will not only have his job I will have his ass."

"Yeah, I guess you're right. You're a better man than I am because I would have kicked his ass, fired him and thought about the consequences later."

"Yeah, you were always the hot head."

"True just like you were always the one who wants to talk and try to work things out with people."

"Have you spoken with Thomas about this?"

"Yes I have. I had a meeting with Thomas and my secretary Patricia. They are the only two that would have access to the company check printer. They both claim not to know anything about the checks nor do they know who this Tony Carter is. The funny thing about the situation is we stopped printing checks a long time ago. I take that back, we have one employee who cannot get a checking account so we still issue him a company payroll check because he refuses to use a pay card. Mr. Jones over at the bank has put an alert out on my accounts just in case this person comes back in and tries to cash another check." Jordan hands the fraud packet to Ronnie. "Mr. Jones gave me this to fill out. He told me that I have to file a police report before the bank will get involved."

"Don't worry about this I will take care of everything for you but you will have to let Mr. Jones know that he will be working with me on your behalf."

"Sure, I'll phone him this morning."

Ronnie continues to examine both sets of checks. It puzzles him because the checks look identical but as he continues to examine them a little closer. He can tell that the fraudulent checks are slightly different. He knows it is not hard to have checks printed using someone else's information. He'll speak with Mr. Jones to find out if Tony Carter's is a bank customer and to talk with the bank teller who cashed these checks. He has a gut feeling that the bank teller is involved.

"How long do you think this will take to find out who's behind this?" Jordan asks.

"Well, it all depends on how helpful Mr. Jones and the bank teller are. Jordan, just in case this is an inside job, your staff cannot know why I am here."

"Alright, I will set you up in the office next to mine and when my staff comes in I will introduce you as my auditor."

Denise Hill

CHAPTER 3

"Now back to you my friend. What is really going on with you? Since I have known you I have never seen you lose focus like this."

"I have something's on my mind right now. This thing with Thomas and Vanessa is bothering me and to be honest with you, I think they are still seeing each other behind my back. I want to fire Thomas so bad I can taste it. Then there is the missing money and to top that, I just found out that Jasmine has moved back and has divorced her husband."

"Are you kidding me?" "That is good news."

"True, that's the best news I have heard in months, but guess what?" "I'm still engaged."

"Come on man, I know you're not going to miss another opportunity to get with Jasmine. I remember when she married that dude and moved to Florida. You moped around here for months, and now she is back and single. Are you going to tell me that you are going to let a woman who cheated on you with the hired help ruin a chance for you to be happy with the person whom you truly love? Man you need to have your head examined," Ronnie says as he shakes his head.

Jordan laughs. He knows deep down inside that Jasmine is the love of his life.

"Since you seem to have all the answers, tell me this. How do you know that Jasmine would even want to see me?"

Ronnie throws up both hands, "I give up. Who told you that Jasmine moved back?"

"Danielle, she called me this morning."

"As smart as I know you are, you are acting pretty dumb right now. Why do you think your sister called this morning to tell you this? Come on man, think. Danielle called to tell you this to get a reaction out of you. She is probably talking with Jasmine, as we speak. You know how your sister is. I can hear her now. "Girl, Jordan was so excited when I told him you had moved back."

Jordan and Ronnie laughed. They know this is probably true.

"Tell me something Jordan. Are you still planning to go through with your crazy idea of marrying Vanessa after all she has put you through?"

"I have thought about this for some time now and to be honest, it has been eating at me. I thought I could deal with it. I tried so hard to forgive her, but I can't. How can I marry a woman who would do this to me? If she did it once, she would probably do it again. I have no respect for her anymore so the answer to your question is no, but before you say anything, NO, I am not calling off the engagement because of Jasmine."

Ronnie knows that this is the perfect reason for Jordan to call off the engagement.

Jordan sets Ronnie up in the office next to his. As his staff strolls in, he introduces Ronnie as his auditor. Jordan's staff seems to take well to Ronnie. They laugh and joke with him and begin to tell him about some of the pranks they have played on Jordan in the past. Ronnie gets the feeling that Jordan's staff loves working for him.

He now understands why Jordan is so devoted to his staff but what he can't understand is why any one of them would steal money from his company. This leads him to believe that Thomas is behind the embezzlement. He just has to prove it.

Ronnie has met everyone except for Thomas. He is aware that Thomas usually comes in around ten.

Vanessa lies in the bed with her eyes closed. This is the second time this week that she has spent the night with Thomas. Vanessa can't understand why she is so drawn to him. Maybe it's because he does things to her sexually that makes her lose control. He is like an addiction she cannot kick but she knows she has to put an end to this before Jordan finds out that she and Thomas have continued to see each other after he caught them in bed together.

Vanessa continues to lay with her eyes closed. She knows Thomas is about to give her that (You need to make up your mind) speech for the tenth time.

Vanessa opens her eyes to find Thomas sitting on the side of the bed. She eases up behind him and starts kissing him softly on his back.

"Baby, what's wrong?"

"Do you have to ask, Vanessa?"

"Oh boy. Here we go again," Vanessa says as she eases off the bed to stand in front of Thomas.

"Look Thomas, I know what I have to do. Please let me handle this my way. I have to find the right time to do this and if you make me choose right now, you may not like the outcome."

Thomas did not say another word. He watches as she makes her way to the bathroom.

Ignoring Thomas's foul mood, she knows she has him right where she wants him, which complicates the situation even more.

Vanessa stands under the shower letting the warm water run down her face and beat up against her body as she thinks about the decision she has to make. Part of her wants to stay with Jordan but her sexual side yearns for Thomas. It is hard for Vanessa to believe that she has allowed herself to get caught up with two men whom she cares so deeply for. In her mind, she begins to weigh the odds with each man when Thomas eases up behind her in the shower. Vanessa turns to face him. They move toward each other. Her breasts push like ripe melons against his chest. She tries ignoring the warm sensation that seeps through her veins, as she looks him dead in his baby blue eyes.

Thomas begins covering her body with her favorite shower gel as he massages every part of her. Vanessa returns the favor covering every inch of him. His eyes fall to her mouth as he groans, unable to contain himself as Vanessa slowly strokes him. She is fascinated with the fullness in her hands. His mouth began to devour hers as he kisses her with all the passion he has, while the water pulses over their bodies. Vanessa gasps as Thomas palms both breast and pushes them together where he beings to lick each nipple simultaneous. He licks his way down her body, stroking her most feminine part of her body with long firm movements of his warm wet tongue while inserting two fingers inside her causing her to explode. Thomas pins her up against the shower wall, force her legs apart with one hand and enters her with one hard thrust.

Vanessa begins rocking her hips, moving her body into his sending tremors all through his body. Thomas begins to moan her name repeatedly as the ripples became a thunderous orgasm that leaves them both weak.

Minutes later when Vanessa's breathing is back to normal, she steps out of the shower, leaving Thomas behind. She grabs a towel wraps it around her body. She glances at herself in the mirror. She knows that if her dad were alive today, he would not be pleased with how she is living her life.

Jordan phones Vanessa at home and gets no answer. He decides against leaving her a message. He figures he can catch her on her cell.

Vanessa is on her way out of the bathroom when she hears her cell phone ringing. She knows it has to be Jordan. Vanessa retrieves her phone from her purse. "Hey baby, how are you this morning?"

"I'm fine Vanessa, I was wondering if I can stop by your place this evening around six, if you're not too busy?"

"Sure, that's fine. That will give me enough time to prepare dinner for you."

"Vanessa, dinner will not be necessary."

"Is there something wrong?

Jordan hesitated before answering, "We will talk about it this evening."

Thomas emerges from the bathroom. He stands in the doorway just in time to hear Vanessa speaking with Jordan.

"I can't believe you!"

Vanessa turns around to find Thomas standing behind her with fire in his eyes. She puts her finger up to her mouth as she backs out of the bedroom hoping Jordan did not hear Thomas in the background.

After Vanessa finishes her conversation with Jordan, she walks back into the bedroom and approaches Thomas, who stands there with his arms folded across his chest.

"How can you be so damn inconsiderate?" Vanessa shouts.

"Inconsiderate, I think you're the one being inconsiderate."

"Oh, really, the way I see it Jordan is still my fiancée or did you forget?"

"I tell you what; if you have not come to a decision by tonight I will make that decision for you." Thomas says as he walks back into the bathroom and slams the door behind him.

Vanessa decides the best thing for her to do is to leave. She is not in the mood to argue with Thomas about a decision he is not going to like. Vanessa gathers her belongings and heads for the guest bedroom as she dresses quickly. She wants to be gone before Thomas comes out.

When Vanessa walks out of Thomas's home, she is a total mess. She closes her eyes as she sits in her car feeling utterly miserable. Wiping away a tear, she tries to smile remembering the good times they shared. She knows Thomas is going to be heartbroken when she calls to give him the news tonight.

~ XXX ~

Denise Hill

CHAPTER 4

Vanessa waits patiently for the elevator. She stands there, so deep in thought that she does not notice the tall handsome man dressed in a dark business suit until the elevator doors opens. The man holds the elevator doors open and allow Vanessa to enter. What she notices about this man makes the hairs on the back of her neck stand straight up. This man looks so much like her dad, who passed away two years ago.

On the elevator ride up Vanessa steals several glances at the stranger from the corner of her eye. She notices his features, which resembles her dad. She has seen pictures of her dad when he was younger and this man could have easily passed for his twin.

The elevator doors open on the 13th floor. Vanessa gets off and so does the stranger. Vanessa makes her way to her secretary's desk to retrieve her messages, "Good morning Jessica. How are you?"

"Good morning, Ms. Cole."

Vanessa sits behind her desk. Her thoughts shifts back to the person she rode up on the elevator with when her secretary knocks at her door.

"Come in," Vanessa says."

"I am sorry to bother you Ms. Cole, but there is a handsome man out front requesting to speak with you. I asked if he had an appointment with you and he said no. He says his name is Jonathan Cole."

"Jonathan Cole," Vanessa says aloud.

"Jessica, would you be so kind to tell Mr. Cole that if he wishes to speak with me, he will have to make an appointment just like everyone else."

Vanessa has no idea that this man is the same man from the elevator.

Vanessa is about to phone Thomas when Mr. Cole burst through the doors with Jessica right behind him. "Ms. Cole, I told him that he had to make an appointment with you."

"That's okay Jessica, I will take it from here."

Vanessa continues to sit behind her desk and stares at the man before her.

"Mr. Cole, do you have a problem with following orders?"

Mr. Cole laughs as he moves further into the room. "No I follow orders just fine. I didn't think I needed to make an appointment with you seeing that this company is just as much mines as it is yours."

"Excuse me," Vanessa says.

"Oh you heard me correctly."

"I have no idea what you're talking about."

Mr. Cole hands Vanessa some documents.

"In my father's will, and there is a copy in those documents, if you need to look it over. It states that our father left his business Cole Laboratory to his children, and the way I see it, I am part owner of this company."

"Mr. Cole, please sit down I think you are confused. My father left this business to me, his only child."

"No, I think you are the one confused. Jonathan Cole was my father. I am his firstborn and I have every legal document to prove it."

Vanessa is shocked. She cannot believe what this man is saying. "Mr. Cole, I do not know what you are trying to pull and I do not care about any documents you have. I know my father had one child and I am that child. Therefore, if you don't mind I have work to do. You can leave the way you came in or I will have security escort you out."

Vanessa reaches for the phone as Mr. Cole slowly walks around to where she is sitting and looks her straight in her eyes. "Vanessa there is no need to call security. I figured we could work this out between us, but I guess I was wrong. Here's my card just in case you decide you want to talk, if not, I will see you in court."

Vanessa sits there in disbelief as Mr. Cole walks out of her office. She cannot believe what just happened. Vanessa decides to look over the documents that Mr. Cole left behind. True enough, she finds a copy of a birth certificate listing Jonathan Cole, Sr. as the father of Jonathan Cole, Jr.

Vanessa picks up the phone to dial her mother. She knows if there is any truth in this, her mother will confirm it.

"Vanessa, calm down and let me explain. Your father had Jonathan six years before we married. Jonathan's mother moved him out of state to spite your dad for marrying me. Your dad tried for years to locate him but was unsuccessful. It tore your dad up inside not being able to see his only son, but when you came along it made it easier on him. As the years went by, your dad stop searching for Jonathan and focused his attention on you. It's true sweetheart, Jonathan Cole is your brother and your father did leave the business to the two of you."

After speaking with her mom, Vanessa is outraged she cannot believe her parents had kept this from her. She had always wanted an older brother, and to find out now, like this that she has one all this time. "Damn you daddy!"

When Thomas comes out of the bathroom, Vanessa is gone. He walks over to his bed where he sits on the edge with his hands up to his face. He has a bad feeling that things are not going to go in his favor with Vanessa. Sadly, he has fallen in love with her something he promised himself he would never do since he knows his family will never accept a black woman into their family.

The rest of the day did not get any better for Thomas. Just as he is settling in, Jordan and Ronnie appear at his door. Jordan introduces Ronnie as his auditor. For the next 15 minutes, they question him about the fraudulent checks. Jordan demands Thomas to turn in his facsimile stamp with Jordan's signature on it and informs him that going forward, he will no longer be authorized to print any payroll checks for James.

By this time, Thomas is nervous as hell. He cannot even look Jordan in the face. He is so consumed with guilt and fear of losing his job.

After leaving Thomas's office, they make a stop at Patricia's desk, Jordan's secretary. They inform her about the changes and request her facsimile stamp as well. Jordan has no reason to believe that Patricia is involved, but to be on the safe side, he has to request her facsimile stamp as well. Ronnie thinks this is the best thing to do until they find the culprit.

Engrossed in his work, Jordan has not noticed the time until a tap at the door interrupts him. "Hey, do you plan on eating lunch anytime soon?" "My stomach has been growling for hours," Ronnie says.

"I'm sorry man. Why didn't you say anything sooner, I normally work through lunch."

"Well, as you can see by my girlish figure, I don't miss any meals."

The two men share a laugh. Jordan shuts off the computer and grabs his jacket.

Jordan and Ronnie stroll down the hall to the elevator. Jordan pushes the down button and waits for the elevator.   As the elevator doors open Jordan steps in, Ronnie hesitates, something about one of Jordan's employees bothers him.

The elevator starts dinging. "Are you coming or not?"

"Yeah, Ronnie steps in and asks Jordan, "What's up with that guy? He seems sort of sneaky to me."

"Roberto is harmless. He is very quiet and usually keeps to himself. Actually, he is one of my best workers."

"I get a bad feeling about him; I will have to keep an eye on him. I swear he was in the hall eavesdropping on our conversation. I guess being a PI you notice things that other people don't normally pick up on."

As the two enter the ground eatery, Jordan hears the growling of Ronnie's stomach. "Man, you were not kidding, I'd bet you could have heard that a mile away."

"Very funny," Ronnie says as the host escorts them to their booth and hands them their menus.

"Your waiter will be out shortly."

After looking over the menu, Ronnie decides to go for the salad bar. Ronnie stands up to leave as the waiter approaches.

"Hello gentlemen. I'm Jason. I will be your waiter today."

"We are going to have the salad bar", Jordan says as he hands the menus to the waiter.

"What can I get you gentlemen to drink?"

"I'll have ice tea with lemon," Jordan replies.

"And what can I get for you sir?"

"I'll take a diet coke."

"Okay, I will be right back with your drinks."

Jordan looks at Ronnie, "Man, I know you are about to pile your plate sky high, and you have the nerve to order a diet coke."

"Man, mind your own business I am a growing man. I need all the food I can get."

"You are crazy, I know that much."

Jordan has already began to eat when Ronnie finally makes it back to the table.

"You should be ashamed of yourself. I am going to talk with Sheila about your eating habits."

"Whatever man, Sheila loves all of this, Ronnie says as he rubs his stomach. "So tell me something Jordan, when are you going to break the news to Vanessa?"

"I'm stopping by her place this evening to tell her."

"I would do anything to be a fly on the wall when you break the news to her."

"I know you would."

"How do you think she's going to take it?"

"She will be angry at first. Then she will think that there's someone else, but then she'll get over it because she will have Thomas and they won't have to sneak around anymore."

"I don't know man. She does not seem like a person who will just get over it that easy."

"Well, that will not be my problem, will it?"

"If you say so, but I know women like that. If they can't have you, they will try to mess up any relationship that you have.

Have you thought anymore about Jasmine and if you're going to pursue her?"

"To be honest with you, I haven't.

"That's bullshit, and you know it."

Jordan could not do anything but laugh. He cannot tell his friend that he has been counting down the days and the hours until he would be in her presence.

"Why don't you finish inhaling your food so we can get back to the office so that you can do what I am paying you to do?"

"Man, I have never seen you this up tight. That woman has done a number on you. She has even gotten you eating like a bird."

"Just for that, lunch is on you."

"That's okay. I'll just add it to your bill."

Jordan shakes his head.

~ xl ~

Denise Hill

CHAPTER 5

Back in his office, Jordan checks his messages. He has one from his mom and two from Vanessa. He has no desire to talk with Vanessa. What he has to say to her will be said this evening.

Jordan picks up the receiver and dials his mom's number.

"Hi mom, I'm sorry I missed your call. Call me when you get in, love you."

Vanessa sits behind her desk trying to focus on the contract that Jared has landed with a new client. She has spent most of the morning unable to concentrate. Vanessa phones Jared and Jordan twice, but both times she gets their voicemail. Seeing that she is not getting anything accomplished, she decides to call it quits for the day. Vanessa grabs her coat, briefcase and makes her way to Jessica's desk.

"Hey Jessica, I'm taking off for the day. Should Jared or Jordan call, can you transfer them to my cell."

"Is everything okay, Ms. Cole?"

"Yes, Jessica. Everything is fine. I will see you in the morning. Vanessa is on her way to her car when her phone rings. Thinking it is Jared or Jordan calling, she quickly pulls her phone from her purse.

"Vanessa this is Thomas, I just called to apologize to you about this morning. I had no right putting you in the situation that I put you in and I am sorry for doing so. I want you to know that I love you dearly, but I also love myself and I can't keep hurting because I can't have you the way I want you so I'm removing myself from the picture. Vanessa, I wish you the best of luck with Jordan. Goodbye Vanessa."

With tears rolling down her face, Vanessa unlocks car door and sits behind the wheel. She tries to stop the tears from coming, but she can't, Thomas is in her system. He is a part of her life and now he is walking away. She thought it would be easy for her to break it off with Thomas, but now that he has done so, it seems as if losing him will be harder than she thought.

Five minutes later, Vanessa is still sitting in the parking garage trying to get a grip on things. She plans on stopping by her mom's for lunch, but she does not want her mom to see her in this condition.

Vanessa arrives at her mom's 25 minutes later. Before getting out of the car, she reaches for the sunglasses on the passenger's seat. There is not an ounce of sun out. It is gloomy exactly how her mood is.

Vanessa's mom meets her at the door.

"Hey sweetie," Vanessa's mom says as she glances at Vanessa and wonders why she is wearing sunglasses.

"Hi mom. How are you?" Vanessa asks as she walks past her mom.

"Why in the world are you wearing sunglasses?"

Vanessa ignores her mother and makes her way to the kitchen.

"I see someone's in a bad mood."

"Mom, I'm sorry I just have a lot on my mind right now."

"Does this have anything to do with Jonathan?"

Vanessa turns to face her mom, "Mom, how could you not tell me about Jonathan. Why did I have to find out this way?"

"Sweetheart I told you, your dad didn't think it would be a good idea."

"Mom, don't you have a mind of your own. Daddy was not always right in the decisions that he made. You could have told me after daddy died, but no, I have to have my brother show up and accuse me and my mother of trying to cheat him out of what is rightfully his."

"Look here missy, don't you come up in my home talking to me with that tone of voice I am not one of your employees."

Vanessa walks over to her mom and wraps her arms around her.

"I'm sorry mom, I really am." Vanessa begins to cry.

"Vanessa baby, what's wrong?"

"Mom, I just lost someone I truly love."

"You and Jordan broke off the engagement?"

"No, someone that I care for deeply is leaving me."

Vanessa sees the confused look on her mom's face.

"Here, why don't you take a seat and I'll prepare some lunch for us and you can tell me all about it."

After lunch, Vanessa and her mom move to the family room where Vanessa explains everything in detail to her mom.

"Vanessa how could you let yourself get caught up in this mess?"

"I don't know Mom it just happened. Thomas and Jordan are very different. There are things that I love about Thomas and then there are things I love about Jordan. I wish I could roll them up into one person then I would have the perfect man."

"Oh Vanessa honey, you know there's no such thing as a perfect man."

"I know mom, but can't I dream?"

"Well, you need to stop dreaming; dreaming is what got you in this mess." You need to come back to reality and make things work with Jordan. Jordan has been faithful to you. Thomas cheated with you, so he will eventually cheat on you."

"Well, I guess I won't have to worry about Thomas anymore."

"Everything happens for a reason Vanessa," her mom says as she holds Vanessa's hands.

"Mom, thanks for listening. I know you're not proud of me right now."

"Baby, everyone makes mistakes. As long as you learn from them. That's the most important thing."

"Well I have to get going; Jordan is stopping by this evening for dinner so I have to stop by the grocery store."

"Alright sweetheart, if you need to talk you know I'm here for you."

"Thanks mom. I love you."

"I love you too, Vanessa."

The afternoon speeds by quickly for Jordan. He is finishing up when he realizes it is five thirty. That will give him only 30 minutes to get to Vanessa's.

Jordan turns off his computer locks his credenza and locks his office door. He walks past Ronnie's office and sticks his head inside.

"You're still here; I thought I was the only one working late."

"Yeah, I'm just finishing up right now."

"Are you sure you don't need me to tag along with you?"

Jordan laughs, "Yes, I'm sure."

"I hope everything goes well," Ronnie says.

Vanessa just finished making dessert when she hears the doorbell. Vanessa washes her hands and dries them on the dishtowel. She checks herself in the mirror in the hallway before opening the door.

"Hey sweetheart, you're just in time." Vanessa says as she greets Jordan with a kiss on the cheek.

"Good evening, Vanessa," Jordan says.

Vanessa hears the coldness in Jordan's voice that causes her to grit her teeth. She knows something is wrong. Jordan removes his coat and lays it across the loveseat.

"Would you like a glass of wine before dinner?" Vanessa asks.

"No thank you. I told you dinner wasn't necessary." Jordan grabs a hold of Vanessa's hand. "We need to sit down and talk."

"Sure," Vanessa says as she allows Jordan to guide her to the couch.

"Is there something wrong Jordan?"

Jordan pauses a moment before speaking,

"Yes, there has been something wrong for a while now."

Vanessa sits waiting for Jordan to speak.

"Vanessa, when I first met you, I thought you were the woman of my dreams. I allowed you to do things to me that no other woman has done. I am sorry to have to do this, but after thinking long and hard about this. I have decided to call off the engagement."

"What! Jordan whatever is troubling you, we can work through this. We can have a nice quiet dinner and afterwards we can talk about whatever is bothering you."

"Vanessa, we are two worlds apart. I don't fit into yours and you don't fit into mine. Trust and honesty means everything to me, but it doesn't seem to mean shit to you. I need someone who will be loyal and who is trustworthy. You have shown me that you are not that person. So I have no other choice but to move on."

Vanessa sits there for a minute or so without saying a word. She is busy trying to digest what Jordan has just said. Jordan continues to sit glancing at Vanessa waiting for a reaction out of her. When he does not get one, he stands and makes his way over to the loveseat and grabs his coat.

"You know what Jordan you are so full of shit. You come over here talking about us being two worlds apart, and that honesty means everything to you. Why don't you be honest right now and tell me the real reason you are breaking up with me."

"I just did."

"No you are lying. Who is she Jordan?"

"What are you talking about who is she?"

"I know there's someone else, Vanessa says."

"I think you're confusing me with yourself, I am not a cheater."

"Why did you waste my time Jordan? You could have told me this shit over the phone. I went through the trouble of cooking dinner for you and making your favorite dessert."

"I wanted to be the mature man that I am and tell you in person. I did not propose to you over the phone so why would I break it off with you over the phone and if I remember correctly, I told you dinner was not necessary."

Jordan heads for the door then does an about-face turning to face Vanessa, "Why don't you call and invite Thomas over for dinner. That's where you were this morning, isn't it?"

Vanessa stands there unable to answer.

"Yeah, that's what I thought. You know you played me once maybe even twice, but you'll never get another opportunity to play me again," Jordan says as he walks out the door.

Vanessa stands and watches as Jordan walks out of her life.

Denise Hill

CHAPTER 6

On the way home, Jordan is relieved. He feels like a huge weight is lifted off his shoulders. Jordan has been going back-and-forth contemplating this decision for weeks. At times, he was not sure if he was just acting out of anger or if it was his bruised ego, but the more he thought about what Vanessa had done, he knows this is what he had to do especially since he learned of Jasmine's return. This news put the icing on the cake. It was the confirmation that he needed.

Jordan arrives home a little after seven that evening. It is too early to call it a night, but he is not up for hanging out. He walks upstairs to the fourth floor to his bedroom. At times like this, he regrets not having the elevator installed. He removes his shoes, throws his jacket across the bed, and unties the tie from his neck. Jordan begins to unbutton his shirt as he walks over to the chaise to grab his sweat pants and T-shirt.

He slips on his slippers that his nephews had given him for his last birthday and makes his way back downstairs.

By the time he reaches the bottom step, his stomach growls. His body is telling him that it is in need of food.

Jordan picks up the phone that is in the hallway and phones Marcos and orders dinner. He orders a small pizza with sausage, pepperoni, mushrooms, onions and extra cheese.

Jordan makes his way to the family room and turns the television on to find something to occupy his mind. He flips through the channels as he comes across the Martin show, which features Brian McKnight. It is the episode where Martin proposes to Gina as Brian McKnight serenades her in the background, singing one of Jordan's favorite songs, Never Felt This Way.

Thoughts of Jasmine began to fill his head. He wonders if he has crossed her mind as much as she has crossed his. Jordan turns the television off, walks over to the bay window in the family room, and stares out into the darkness. He muses about his life as he saw it and as he wanted it to be.

He has to be honest with himself. He wants Jasmine more than ever. He tries his best to keep his thoughts away from her, but no matter how hard he tries, he can't help himself. This woman is in his system and has been for a very long time. Jasmine is special. He watched her grow from a scrawny little girl into a beautiful woman, a woman he plans to make his. The sound of the doorbell interrupts his thoughts. Jordan makes his way to the door grabbing his wallet off the coffee table.

"Good evening Mr. Daniels."

"Good evening Bob. How are you?"

"I'm hanging in there," Bob replies.

Jordan hands Bob a twenty-dollar bill in exchange for the pizza.

"Keep the change Bob and have a good evening."

"Thanks, Mr. Daniels."

Jordan grabs two beers from the refrigerator and sits by the fireplace eating and listening to the sound of soft jazz. He listens to the music as the whistling of the wind blows against the shutters. This would be a good night to cuddle by the fireplace with someone special, Jordan thinks.

After Jordan's departure, Vanessa phones her cousin Jared at his hotel. She left a message earlier that day, but he has yet to call. Vanessa tries calling his cell phone again but it goes straight to voicemail.

"Jared, where the hell are you, I need to talk with you as soon as possible." After several attempts, Vanessa is still unsuccessful in reaching Jared.

For the rest of the evening, Vanessa sits in her recliner, intent on relaxing with a cup of coffee and a novel she had bought a week ago. Vanessa tries her best to clear her mind of today's event and focus on her novel, but she is unsuccessful. She has lost her appetite and can't focus as the truth sinks through. The thought of her not having Jordan in her life is something she is not going to take well. She has to come up with a plan to win Jordan back.

~ liv ~

An hour later, Vanessa's phone rings, thinking it is Thomas, she decides to let the answering machine pick up the call. After four rings, the familiar male voice comes through the speaker, "Vanessa, this is Jared, I'm sorry I missed your calls."

Vanessa rushes to the phone. "Jared, I am so glad you finally decided to return my calls, we have a big problem." Vanessa explains everything to Jared about Jonathan. "Vanessa don't do anything until I get back. My plane arrives Wednesday afternoon. I will come straight to the office. Don't worry. Everything will be fine, I promise."

When Vanessa gets off the phone with Jared, she does not feel any better than she did before. Vanessa wants to call Jordan and talk with him about it, but she decides against it. She wants to give Jordan some time to think about what happened earlier. She knows eventually he will come to his senses and come crawling back to her, at least this is what she hopes for, but the one thing that she does not know is Jordan's true love has moved back to town and he has plans of rekindling what they shared years ago.

Jordan opens his eyes and looks around the room when he realizes he has fallen asleep on the coach. He glances at the clock on the wall. It reads 11 o'clock. He gathers the empty pizza box and the two empty beer cans and toss them in the trashcan in the kitchen.

Before heading upstairs, he sets the alarm and turns out the lights.

In his bedroom too tired to shower, he dress down to his boxers and buries himself underneath his comforter. Jordan tosses and turns for hours trying to get the images of Jasmine out of his head until sleep falls upon him. The next morning, Jordan rises early he stretches as he gets out of bed and brace himself for the day. Little does he know that in less than 72 hours, his life will change forever.

Jordan staggers downstairs to the kitchen where the smell of brewing coffee greets him. Jordan pours himself a cup of coffee and sits there for the next 30 minutes at the kitchen table watching the morning news.

Jordan steps off the elevator where his staff greets him with smiles and looks of approval. His staff has never seen him dress casual before. They didn't even know he owned a pair of jeans.

"Hey, what's up with you guys? Can't a man were a pair jeans every now and then?" he asks his staff.

"Yeah, Mr. D is just that you look so different in jeans," one of Jordan's interns replies.

Ronnie stands at the end of the hall smiling.

"What's up with you?" Jordan asked.

"Oh, nothing. It just amazes me how the opposite sex reacts to you."

~ lvi ~

"And how is that?"

"Come on man, you see how the women look at you when you enter a room. I have to give it to you brother you are still as smooth as you were in college."

Jordan looks at Ronnie and shakes his head. Ronnie follows Jordan into his office and shuts the door behind him.

"All right let's hear it. How did it go with Vanessa, yesterday?"

"It went better than I expected. She never saw this coming, she had no clue that I know she is still seeing Thomas behind my back. I said what I have to say and I was out of there."

"Did you speak with your sister last night?"

"No, I told you I was not going to call her and ask her anything about Jasmine. Danielle has always told me that Jasmine was the person I should have been with. I don't need to hear I told you so."

Ronnie chuckles, "Your sister is a trip."

"Tell me about it."

"I hate to change the subject, but I have an appointment today with the Banking Center manager at one. "Would you like to come along?"

"No, that's not necessary I'll let you do what you do best, besides I will only be in the office until about two today. So if you need me call me on my cell."

"You mean you are leaving work early?"

Jordan smiles as he looks at Ronnie.

"Yes, I have something to take care of."

"Oh, I see," Ronnie says."

Denise Hill

CHAPTER 7

Ronnie arrives 10 minutes early for his appointment. As he waits in the lobby, he notices that there are security cameras.   He makes a note to ask Mr. Jones about the videotape.

Ronnie continues to wait until a tall slender man with salt and pepper hair approaches him.

"Good afternoon sir, I'm Mr. Jones. I take it you're Mr. Taylor?" Ronnie stands to shake the older man's hand.

"Yes, I'm Mr. Taylor."

"Why don't you follow me into my office?"

Inside his office, Mr. Jones points to the roundtable. "Let us sit down. Would you care for anything to drink before we get started?"

"No, thank you."

Mr. Jones opens a manila folder. "I made copies of the checks in questioned, I also made copies of Mr. Daniels bank statements. It looks like the same teller cashed each check Toni Reynolds who is one of our floaters."

"What is a floater?" Ronnie asks.

"A floater is a person who does not work at a particular location. They rotate their days at each banking center. She is normally at our banking center twice a month."

"Do you think it's possible that she could be in on this?"

"Anything is possible."

"Have you spoken to her about the checks?"

"No, I haven't. We have not been able to reached Toni. She has been on vacation for the last two weeks and is due back to work soon.

We were going to question her then, but in the meantime, we took precautions regarding Mr. Daniels accounts with us." Mr. Jones hands Ronnie a card with the teller's name and phone number.

"I notice the cameras in the lobby, how often is the film changed?"

"We try and change it every other day. I took the liberty of ordering the video tapes on the days the checks were cashed. I should have those within a week or so, once they come in, I will contact you so that you can come down and pick them up.

I also put an alert out on the accounts to let the tellers know that there has been fraudulent activity on this account and that they should call Mr. Daniels and get his approval before cashing any checks."

"What happens if you are unable to contact Mr. Daniels?"

"Then the tellers will not be able to cash the checks."

"Is it possible for you to notify me if you're unable to contact Mr. Daniels?"

"Yes, we can do that, but I will need something in writing from Mr. Daniels giving us permission to contact you in his absence."

"I will make sure that Mr. Daniels gets something to you in writing. In the meantime, I will try to contact Toni Reynolds to see if she can tell me anything about the person who came in to catch these checks. Is Tony Carter a bank customer?"

"No, we have checked our records and were not able to come up with any information on this individual."

"Do you normally cash checks for that large amount of money without that person having an account with you?"

"No not at all. Toni Reynolds has been with the bank for years and knows the procedure so I can't say why she would have cashed these checks."

"Alright then, I guess this will be all for right now," Ronnie says as he stands and reaches his hand out to shake Mr. Jones hand.

"I want to thank you for taking time out of your busy schedule to meet with me."

"It was my pleasure. I would do anything for Mr. Daniels."

After meeting with Mr. Jones for forty-five minutes, Ronnie makes it back just in time to talk with Jordan before he leaves for the day.

"How did it go with Mr. Jones?"

Ronnie explains everything that they had discussed in the meeting.

"Well, if you don't need anything else I'm heading home," Jordan says.

"No, go-ahead I am going to hang around here for awhile. I need to contact Toni Reynolds to see if she can tell me anything about Tony Carter. Oh, I almost forgot, you will need to fax over a letter to Mr. Jones giving him permission to contact me in your absence in case someone comes into the bank and tries to cash another check. I will also need a list of issued checks, so I have a list to go by."

"I'll have Patricia get a letter together for you tomorrow. I guess I will see you in the morning, have a nice evening," Jordan said.

Roberto hurries off before he is caught listening behind closed doors. He cannot be sure how much Ronnie knows about Toni Reynolds involvement. Therefore, he has to get to her before Ronnie does.

Ronnie goes back to his office. He sits behind his desk and looks over the card that Mr. Jones has given him. He picks up the phone and dials Toni's number. It rings four times before the answer machine kicks in. Ronnie hangs up. He decides to try to phone her later that evening.

Jordan arrives home just as Alexis pulls up. Today is her first day as Jordan's housekeeper. Alexis took on the part-time job not because she needs the extra money, but to be closer to Jordan.

After several conversations with his mom about hiring someone to come in and clean his home three days a week, Jordan decides to take out an ad in the local newspaper for a part-time housekeeper. The next day a staff member informs him that Alexis is interested in the position. Four years ago, Alexis worked for Jordan as a temp while his secretary was out on medical leave. While there, she made friends with some of Jordan's staff. She continued to keep in touch with them after her assignment ended. This is how she learned of Jordan's need for a housekeeper. He remembers the exceptional job that she had done and hired her over the phone.

Alexis works four hours a day at Community Hospital in housekeeping. Over the years, Alexis has done pretty well for herself. After her grandparents died, she along with her older brother inherited their grandparent's home, along with $150,000 each, which they invested wisely in stocks and mutual funds. Therefore, money is not an issue for her. Alexis is very conservative, she drives a 2004

Honda accord and save every penny that she earns, while her brother lives lavishly and drives a 2007 black Lexus.

Jordan stands outside of his front door as Alexis walks up the walkway. Threading her fingers through her long black tousled hair, she smiles as she greets Jordan.

Alexis follows Jordan inside, she notices the way Jordan's jeans fit his body. In the six months that she worked for Jordan, she had never seen him in anything other than a suit.

"I stopped by the store to buy some cleaning supplies that I thought you might need. Let me know if there's anything that I may have forgotten."

Jordan gives Alexis a tour of his home. He shows her his office and makes it clear that she is never to enter his office and that this room is off limits to everyone. His office is where he keeps his safe and very important documents that if they got in the hands of the wrong person it could destroy everything he has worked so hard to get.

At the end of the tour, Alexis is amazed, she cannot believe that someone who has it so good can be so down to earth.

"Alexis, I don't expect you to work today, I just wanted you to see what you were getting yourself into. You haven't changed your mind, have you?"

"Jordan please, a little work has never hurt anyone." "Oh before forget, I will need a key to the house."

Jordan pulls a key out of his jean pocket. "I have it right here." Come follow me. I need to show you how to work the alarm system."

Jordan is showing Alexis the alarm system when his stomach growls.

"It sounds as if your stomach is telling you something, Jordan."

"Yeah, I skipped lunch today.

"Jordan. That is not healthy for you. Why don't I throw something together for you?"

"Alexis, I didn't hire you to be my cook."

"I know you did not, but since I am here, I would be more than happy to prepare dinner for you."

Alexis heads for the kitchen and grabs the apron that is hanging on the door. She walks over to the refrigerator opens the door and grabs the package of chicken breast.

Jordan walks in the kitchen behind her, "Alexis, really you do not have to do this."

"I know I don't have to, but I want to."

~ lxvi ~

"Well if you insist, I will go up and shower. If you need anything just press the intercom over there."

CHAPTER 8

After preparing dinner, Alexis stands at the bottom of the stairs to see if Jordan is anywhere in sight. Once she sees the coast is clear she heads for his office, but before she has a chance to turn the knob, the phone rings startling her.

Alexis did not know if she should answer the phone or let the answering machine pick up the call. On the fourth ring, Alexis picks up the phone, "Hello, the Daniels residence."

"Who is this?"

"This is Alexis, who is this?"

"This is Vanessa". Where is Jordan?"

"Jordan is in the shower right now."

"Who the hell are you?"

"I'm Jordan's new housekeeper."

"Housekeeper, yeah right, just have Jordan give me a call when he gets out of the shower," Vanessa says before hitting the end button. She tosses the phone in the passenger sit in frustration.

Vanessa has been sitting in her car parked down the street. She watched Jordan and Alexis enter the house. She knows there was a reason other than what Jordan told her for their breakup.

45 minutes later, Jordan heads downstairs as the doorbell rings. He opens the door to find Vanessa fuming.

"Who the hell is Alexis?"

"What, what are you talking about?"

"I called over here and someone answered your phone. Is she the reason you broke off our engagement?"

Aren't you a little old to be keeping company with someone so young?"

"Vanessa, Alexis is my new housekeeper, and you know damn well she is not the reason I broke off our engagement. Look Vanessa, this is my house and I will decide who comes and goes. It really isn't any of your business anymore so the next times you want to run up in here making accusations please remember that."

"Jordan, your dinner is ready," Alexis yells from the kitchen. Vanessa looks at Jordan before walking past him down the hall to the kitchen where Alexis is sitting at the kitchen table.

Jordan is right on her heels because he knows how Vanessa can be.

~ lxx ~

Vanessa stands there with her hands on her hips taking in every inch of Alexis.

"Did you give Jordan my message?"

"I'm sorry, who are you?"

"Bitch you know who I am!"

"Hold up, Jordan says as he steps in front of Vanessa. You will not come into my home and disrespect my guest."

"I left a message with her telling you to call me. Did you get that message?" Vanessa shouts.

"No, I didn't."

"That's what I thought."

"Vanessa, I was in the shower and was heading downstairs when you rang the doorbell. Alexis has not had time to tell me anything. You need to apologize to her."

"Please, apologize my ass! You broke off our engagement so that you could play house with this little tramp."

"That's it. I want you to leave."

Jordan grabs Vanessa by the arm and walks her to the door. "Vanessa you are not welcome here anymore until you learn to respect my guests," Jordan says as he opens the front door.

"Jordan, how could you do this to me? I thought I meant something to you."

"You did at one time, but when you slept with Thomas, that changed everything."

"I thought you forgave me for that?" Vanessa says as tears roll down her face.

"I did, I just couldn't forget it."

"I love you so much Jordan, I don't want to spend the rest of my life without you."

"Vanessa please, you do not know the meaning of love," Jordan says as he closes the door.

Jordan walks back into the kitchen where he finds Alexis sitting at the kitchen table. She has prepared chicken breast with macaroni and cheese, fried potatoes and fried biscuits.

"I'm sorry Jordan. I didn't have a chance to tell you she called."

"Don't you dare apologize for anything. You did nothing wrong. I want to apologize to you for Vanessa's behavior. I guess you should know since you will be around Vanessa and I were engaged. I broke it off with her yesterday and now she is trying to find any reason she can come up with it as to why I called it off.

When in fact, she is the reason I called it off. If she ever comes around here again and I am not here, whatever you do, do not let her in."

"Well, you won't have to worry about that. She acted like a mad woman."

Jordan chuckles.

Jordan sits down at the kitchen table and looks at his plate.

"How did you prepare this meal so quick?"

Alexis smiles. "When you know what you're doing in the kitchen it doesn't take a long time to prepare a meal."

"I know I couldn't have prepared this in less than an hour."

"If you ever want me to cook dinner for you just let me know."

"I didn't hire you to cook Alexis."

"I know, I don't mind, in fact, I love to cook."

"Well since you put it that way. I might take you up on your offer sometime.

20 minutes later, Jordan and Alexis are standing at the kitchen sink doing the dishes. Alexis washes the dishes while Jordan dries them. "Alexis what are your plans for the holiday?"

"My brother and I are going to Atlanta to visit my aunt and uncle."

"Are you guys driving?"

"No, we decided to fly this time. Neither one of us is up for the long drive. Our plane leaves tomorrow at 1:30 PM."

"Yeah, that would be a long drive."

"Do you have any family here besides your brother?"

"No, my brother and I are the only ones here. We have family in Atlanta, Ohio, St. Louis, Tennessee and California. Our family is scattered all over, but that's a good thing, because we get to travel every holiday and whenever we go to visit we never have to get a hotel. There is always enough room for everyone. I love the holidays because I get to spend time with my family. Now my brother would prefer to stay at home for the holidays. The holiday's hasn't always been good for him ever since my dad died years ago."

"Were they close?"

"You know, what I can remember they were always at each other's throat, but he seems to have taken my dad's death harder than anyone."

"If you're leaving tomorrow you should get going on."

"I know I haven't even packed."

Jordan looks at Alexis and shakes his head.

"Women, why do you guys wait until the last minute to pack when you've known for weeks that you're going out of town?"

"I guess I'm a procrastinator."

"I would say so."

"Well, I couldn't leave you with this mess to clean up."

"And why not, you cooked, the least I can do is do my own dishes."

"Well, everything is finished now so stop complaining," Alexis said as she playfully punched Jordan in the arm.

"You didn't tell me you had a violent side," Jordan says as he pretends to be hurt.

"Jordan you're a mess. Let me grab my things so that I can get out of your hair."

"Let me walk you out to your car." Jordan puts down the dish towel and hangs the apron up.

"If you insist, you know I'm a big girl I can make it to my car by myself."

Jordan chuckles. She is something else, he thinks to himself.

Jordan walks Alexis to her car. As she approaches the driver's side, she notices the door has a scratch from the front to the back.

"Oh my God, Alexis yells. Look at my car; I can't believe someone has keyed my car!"

"What, are you sure it wasn't like this before you got here?"

"Yes, I am sure; I just have my car washed today, and there was not a scratch anywhere."

"I am sorry Alexis, when you get back I want you to go and get an estimate on how much this will cost to buff the scratch out and I'll take care of it."

"Jordan, you do not have to do this. This is not your fault."

"I know, but it happened on my property, and I have a pretty good idea as to who did this", Jordan says.

"All right, Jordan, thank you."

"No, thank you for agreeing to work as my housekeeper, and thanks for dinner."

"Have a safe trip."

"Thanks Jordan, and Happy Thanksgiving."

Jordan stands on the sidewalk until Alexis car is out of sight.

Denise Hill

CHAPTER 9

The next morning Jordan rise from his bed shortly after seven and heads for the shower. The warm water did little to take his mind off the reason he was unable to sleep. It was over 15 years ago, that he had an encounter with Jasmine. His memory of their first kiss is as vivid as if it happened last night. Over the years, Jordan had encountered many women, but no one ever touch him the way Jasmine had. He had not been intimate with her perhaps that was the reason she hunts him in his dreams.

Standing under the spray, he rinsed the soap off his body. He has to figure out a way to get his emotions under control when it comes to Jasmine.

Shutting off the water, he grabs a towel and slowly runs it over his body.

Tossing the towel into the open hamper, he walks over to the drawer and pulls out a pair of Calvin Klein boxers. He lotions his body down and then slips on a tan sweater and a pair of Sean John jeans.

After Jordan finishes dressing, he hooks his cell phone onto his pants and makes his way downstairs for cup of coffee.

On his way to work, Jordan stops at the local supermarket. Every year at Thanksgiving and Christmas time, he always presents his staff with a gift certificate for a turkey or ham. This is just one of his many ways to say thank you and to let them know that he really appreciates everything they do.

Jordan remembers how Thanksgiving was for his family after their father passed away. Some years they had a turkey and some years they could not afford to buy one. Jordan wants to make sure his staff has one every year.

Vanessa wakes the next morning feeling more miserable than she had felt the day before. She did not realize that losing Jordan is like losing a part of herself. Jordan is not perfect, but he is the best man she has ever had and probably would ever have. Vanessa continues to chastise herself for betraying Jordan but what was done is done and now she needs to find a way to win Jordan back.

Vanessa glances at the clock on her nightstand. It is seven in the morning, time to get her day started, but today she has no desire to go into the office. She reaches for the phone to leave her secretary a voice message that she will not be in and wishes her a Happy Thanksgiving.

Jared's plane lands on scheduled. After retrieving his luggage, he catches the shuttle to his car. He feels bad not telling Vanessa about Jonathon before contacting him. At the time, he thought he was doing the right thing by bringing brother and sister together he never imagine Jonathan would accuse Vanessa and her mom of trying to keep his part of the business from him.

Jared arrives at the office to find out that Vanessa has stayed home today. Jared walks to his office, grabs the phone, and dials Vanessa's number.

"Hey Vanessa, are you okay? You don't sound good."

"Jared my life is falling apart, Vanessa says as she begins to cry and tries to explain that Jordan has called off their engagement.

"Vanessa calm down, I am on my way over."

Jared arrives at Vanessa's in record time. He uses the key that Vanessa had given him when she moved in. Jared and Vanessa were more like brother and sister instead of first cousins. Jared's mother and Vanessa's dad were brother and sister. They lived two doors down from Vanessa and her family ever since they were toddlers. They grew up together hanging out with the same crowd and they even went to the same college.

Jared has been there for Vanessa through good and bad times and has helped her get through some tough times in her life. He loves her like a sister and would do anything for her.

Jared's entry startles Vanessa, "Oh my God, you scared the daylights out of me."

"I 'm sorry. I guess I should have knocked first."

Jared walks over and takes a seat next to Vanessa on the couch. "Vanessa I think I need to explain something to you about Jonathan. You may hate me for my decision, but at the time your mom and I thought this was best for both Jonathan and you."

Vanessa looks at Jared through her tear-filled eyes as he begins to explain. "I contacted Jonathan a couple of months ago and ask him if he would come to town to meet you. I had no idea he would accuse you and your mom of keeping his part of the business from him."

"What, you mean to tell me that you are the reason for all of this?"

"Hear me out Vanessa before you blow up. Out of respect, I obeyed your dad's wishes and never told you about your brother. I disagreed with your dad's decision to keep Jonathan a secret from you. The years went by the more you complained about being an only child, I took that role as your brother but now it is time for me to take a step back and let you have that relationship that you always wanted with your real brother.

Your mom and I agreed that this is for the best. I also agree to step down as VP and let Jonathan have his rightful place in the company."

Now that Jared has gotten that off his chest, he waits for a response from Vanessa he knows she is fuming.

Vanessa continues to sit in silence.

"Are there anymore secrets that I do not know about?" she asks Jared as she gets up from the couch.

"No Vanessa."

Vanessa heads for the kitchen, but stops she turns to face Jared while pointing her finger at him.

"You know what, I feel betrayed by the two people that I thought cared about me more than anyone. Now I know how Jordan feels. Jordan broke off our engagement because I betrayed him by sleeping with Thomas and now Thomas broke it off with me. You know I am tired, I am so tired of everything that has been happening in my life."

Jared remains seated on the couch. He feels bad and he knows Vanessa is hurting. Vanessa is not as strong as people believe her to be.

"Vanessa," Jared says as he makes his way into the kitchen. He holds his arms open and Vanessa walks into his embrace where she breaks down.

"I am so sorry to hear about you and Jordan. I am sorry about contacting Jonathan without your permission. You know I would never do anything to hurt you. I just thought I was doing the right thing. I'll call and speak with Jonathan, in the meantime, I want you to pull yourself together. It's not the end of the world."

"That's easy for you to say because you are not the one who has been dumped by two people that you care about."

Jared did not want to go there with Vanessa because he had tried to tell her to leave Thomas alone anyway. He knew that Thomas's family was prejudice and would never accept her.

"Why don't I invite Jonathan over for Thanksgiving so that the two of you can get to know each other? How does that sound?"

"That doesn't sound too good right now. I am not in the mood to deal with him."

"Vanessa this is not like you. You better snap the hell out of this funky mood." Jared says as he snaps his fingers in the air and rolls his neck as he has seen many gay people do. Vanessa had to laugh.

"Jared why aren't you at work?"

"I had to come over and make sure that my favorite girl is alright."

"I am so glad to have you in my life. I don't know what I would do without you."

"Well you know we have been through so much together and we both manage to come out on top." Jared hangs around little bit longer then he leaves and promises to make things right with Jonathan.

"Hey Mr. D, what are your plans for the holidays?" One of Jordan's staff asks as Jordan hands out the gift certificates.

"Same as every year my siblings and I gather at my Moms. If I don't see guys before you leave, have a Happy Thanksgiving."

Jordan sits in his office; he is looking forward to his family's Thanksgiving tradition even more this year. Every year since his siblings moved out, his family always gathers at his moms on Thanksgiving eve.

The women go grocery shopping while the men stay at home with the kids. They usually ordered pizza and play video games with them.

Jordan is going over the monthly budget that Thomas had turned in yesterday. Jordan is going to be out on vacation for a week so he wants to make sure he has everything completed before he leaves.

Jordan looks up when he hears a knock at his door. He looks up to find Roberto standing there.

"I'm sorry to bother you, Mr. Daniels, but I was wondering would it be okay if I took off today at 10. I have a plane to catch at 1:30 and I need to pack."

Jordan laughs. He thought about Alexis and the comment that he made about women being procrastinators.

"Sure, Roberto, that's fine there's not a lot going on here anyway. Have a Happy Thanksgiving and have a safe trip. I'll see you when you return."

"Thanks boss, Happy Thanksgiving." No, sooner than Roberto leaves Jordan's office, his private line rings, fearing it is Vanessa, he lets it go to voicemail. He is not in the mood to deal with Vanessa. She is in his past and that is where he wants to keep her.

CHAPTER 10

DANIELLE AND DONNIE

It is Wednesday, Thanksgiving Eve. How is Danielle going to tell her family that she kicked her husband out. Donnie has been a part of her family's life since forever. The kids are sad and missing their dad and Danielle is hurt and angry that Donnie would do something like this. They have had problems before, but it has never gotten to the point where he cheated.

Six days ago, Donnie and Danielle just had a big fight Friday night.

Danielle storms out of the house. She needs to get away before she says something she would later regret, but little does she know what life has in store for her.

Brenda is sitting at the dining room table as she watches Donnie and Danielle argue. She has been waiting for this opportunity and it has finally come. She has to find a way to make Donnie see that she is the one that he needs. Danielle is her friend, but she could not let that friendship stand in her way of happiness. True enough, Danielle has been there for her. She invited her into her home to live when she had nowhere else to go.

Brenda approaches Donnie as he stands looking out the window as Danielle drives off.

"Donnie she will be back. She just needs time to think about things."

"Right now, I don't give a damn if she comes back or not."

"Do you really mean that Donnie?"

Donnie wipes his hand across his face, and turns to look at Brenda.

"I'm sorry that you had to be here to witness this. We have had arguments in the past, and we have said some hurtful things that we did not really mean, but tonight things were different. There was so much anger in the both of us. I am so glad that the boys were at their grandmothers. I never want them to see their parents argue like this."

"Well Donnie, if it makes you feel any better, I think you were right to say what you said. She has not been here for you or the boys since she got that promotion. It makes me wonder what's more important."

"Well, I'm glad someone else sees my side of it. At first I thought it was just me, but you noticed it too."

"Yes, I have noticed many things Donnie. Why don't you have a seat on the couch and I'll grab a couple of beers for us both. It's good to talk out your frustrations with someone who doesn't take sides."

Within two hours, Donnie and Brenda have consumed eight beers. Donnie is not a drinker and Brenda knows this. This was all part of her scheme to get him in bed with her.

Danielle drives around for hours. Still angry and not wanting to go home. She decides to get a hotel room for the night.

Inserting the key card into the slot, Danielle waits for the green signal and pushes open the door. The room is small, but it would serve its purpose. She drops her purse near the closet and turns to slide the security latch into place.

Before she ever has a chance to settle in her cell phone begins to ring. She decides to let it go to voicemail. Danielle kicks off her shoes and lay across the bed, as her breathing deepens, her eyelids flutters until she is fast asleep.

Brenda walks Donnie to his bedroom. He undresses down to his boxers turns the light out and flops into bed.

Brenda waits a while before entering the room. She waits to make sure Donnie is asleep.

Minutes later, Brenda makes her way back into his room. She slowly undresses herself and eases in bed next to him. She has plans of seducing Donnie and falling asleep in bed with him in hopes of Danielle coming home to catch them. This is the only way to assure her that Donnie and Danielle marriage will be over.

Donnie is knocked out he has no idea what is going to happen and how this will change his life forever.

Brenda eases down his boxers as she places Donnie's penis in her mouth, she works her magic until it becomes long and hard. Donnie awakes to the sensation running through his body. He begins to move and starts to moan thinking its Danielle. He pulls her closer to his face as he devours her mouth he works his way down to her breasts as he takes one of her nipples into his mouth. Brenda takes hold of Donnie's face and kisses every inch of his face. She moves down to his chest where she lets her tongue run over his nipple before taking it into her mouth. Then she begins to plant tiny kisses down his body before she comes to his pole and inserts it back into her mouth. Unable to take any more Donnie pulls her on top of him and inserts himself inside of her. Brenda gives the Donnie the ride of his life until they both explode and fall fast asleep in each other's arms.

Danielle has been sleep for a couple of hours when the sound of laughter outside her door wakes her. She glances at her cell phone. It is 3:30 in the morning. She decides to go home and make things right with her husband. Donnie is right. She has been slacking on her duties since she got her promotion and has been taking advantage of Brenda's kindness to fill in for her.

Danielle wants to tell Donnie that she is sorry about their fight and that things will be different from now on. Danielle checks out of the hotel and is on her way

~ XC ~

home. When she arrives, she notices the front door slightly open. She enters the house, slips off her coat and shoes, lays her purse on the counter, and makes her way to their bedroom.

Danielle was unprepared at what she was about to see. She flicks the light switch on to find Donnie and Brenda asleep in their bed naked.

"What the hell is going on?" Danielle yells.

Donnie and Brenda both jumped at the sound of Danielle's voice. Danielle runs toward Donnie and with all her might, she throws a punch that lands against his jaw. Donnie grabs Danielle to keep her from swinging on him again. Danielle breaks loose from Donnie. She heads for Brenda when Donnie jumps in her path and takes the blow that is meant for her.

"Donnie I want your ass out of my house right now and take this bitch with you!"

"Danielle sweetheart, let me explain, this is not what you think, I have no idea how she ended up in bed with me."

"Let you explain my ass. How could you not know she was in bed with you naked?"

"It was the beers Donnie cried. I had four beers and you know I'm not a drinker."

"Then why were you drinking?"

"I was upset about our fight. Brenda thought this would help ease my mind."

Danielle looks at Brenda if looks could kill, Brenda would be dead.

"You are such a bitch. I bring you into my home when you had nowhere else to go and this is the thanks I get."

"Don't blame me. You're the one that wasn't taking care of your husband so I had to fulfill his needs."

"Danielle baby it was nothing like that, Brenda how can you say that?"

"Donnie, you said it yourself that she wasn't taking care of her duties. Don't go trying to change your story now that you got caught. I didn't hear you say anything about Danielle when I had your dick in my mouth or when I was riding you," Brenda says as she gathers her clothes.

Danielle rushes over to Brenda and grabs her by her hair as she throws her down on the bed and starts punching her.

Donnie runs over and grabs Danielle. "This is crazy baby. You know I would never do anything to hurt you. I was drunk and that is the only reason this happened."

"Drunk or not, I want the both of you out of here before I do something that I will later regret."

Danielle has not heard from Donnie since that dreadful morning. This year the holidays will be different for her and the boys.

Guilt surged out of every pore of Donnie's body as he sits on the side of the bed in his hotel room. It has been six days and he has not spoken to his boys. He misses them so much he misses Danielle even more, but he did not have enough guts to pick up the phone to call them. Donnie continues to sit feeling sorry for himself when he hears a knock at the door. Donnie peeps through the keyhole. He opens the door when he sees it is Brenda. Brenda stands there with her luggage.

"Brenda what are you doing here? I thought you were going to stay with your mom."

"I was staying with her, but I could not stand to hear one more of her lectures. I thought I could just stay here with you until we figure out what we are going to do."

"What do you mean, until we figure out what we are going to do?"

"I already know what I'm going to do I am going to get my wife and my kids back."

"What!" Brenda yells as she moves in front of Donnie. "You are so weak. Danielle does not want you. Can't you see that? I am the one who wants you. I have been taking care of you for the last three months or did you forget that? Danielle has been so occupied with her job that she has deprived you and the boys."

"Brenda just shut the hell up. This is your fault. Was this your plan from the start for Danielle to catch us in bed so that you could ruin my marriage? If this was your crazy little plan I've got news for you, it will not work."

"Donnie, what is it going to take for you to see that Danielle doesn't love you anymore? She has told me that on numerous occasions. Do you think she has really been working all those long hours? Come on Donnie, you're not stupid."

"Alright Brenda, you have one more time to say something stupid like that and you are out of here."

"I'm sorry Donnie if the truth hurts you."

"That's it! Get your belongings and get the hell out of my hotel room!"

"Donnie please, I'm so sorry I had no right to tell you things that your wife told me in confidence. Please forgive me. Brenda continues to tell Donnie how sorry she is and that she only wants the best for him. It had taken some doing but Brenda believes she has been successful in getting Donnie to believe he needs her. She was his friend, lover, and confidant.

Denise Hill

CHAPTER 11

Danielle and the boys are the first to arrive at her moms. She wants to get there before everyone else. She needs to talk to her mom alone to explain the situation between Donnie and her.

Minutes later, the whole gang is there. The women gather in the kitchen putting together their grocery list, while the men gather in the family room with the kids.

"Danielle, why you don't make that peanut butter cake that Jordan likes so much, Mrs. Daniels asks."

"It's already on my list Mom." Danielle says with much sadness in her voice.

"Monica do you have Macaroni and cheese on your list?"

"Yes I do Mrs. Daniels. I'm going to fix it a little different from last year, but I guarantee you guys will love it."

"I have no doubt about that. Matthew is constantly bragging about your cooking. No wonder my boy is getting a potbelly on him."

"Don't blame that on me that's coming from him hanging out with the boys drinking beer at those football games."

"I know that's right," Loretta chimes in.

"All right ladies, it looks like we have everything written down. Let's hit the road before everyone buys up everything," Mrs. Daniels says.

By the time Danielle makes it home and puts the boys to bed, it is ten o'clock. She sits in the family room by the fireplace wondering how things have gotten to this point. "I had to have seen this coming." Getting up she stands by the patio one shoulder resting against the sliding glass door. She has not felt so alone since ten years ago when Donnie and her separated for a year. That was the worse year of her life and now it seems as if she is about to relive it again.

Danielle thought being around her family would ease the pain but Donnie was a part of her family and has been for years. Donnie and Danielle started dating at the age of fifteen. They had been good friends before they decided to take it to the next level. They just recently celebrated their 17th anniversary two months ago. No one could have told her that Donnie would have cheated on her after all of these years, but realization settles in, not too long ago she almost had an affair.

Danielle turns away from the patio knowing time is running out for them especially with Brenda in the picture. She has to do something to get her husband back, only if it were as simple as that. Donnie has not even bothered to call his boys and that is not like Donnie to be away from them and not call.

It was one o'clock in the morning when Danielle turns out the lights in the family room and makes her way down the hall to their bedroom. She pulls back the comforter and sheet and lays down as emotions of fatigue and sadness war with each other as she collapse into a deep sleep.

Donnie sits parked outside his home for hours. He misses his boys and his wife. He cannot imagine his life without them. Donnie watches as the lights go out in the family room he would give anything to cuddle up next to Danielle as she sleeps. He thinks about sneaking in the house and easing into their bed beside her but he does not know how she would react so he decides to head back to his hotel room.

The next morning Danielle lays in bed in deep thought when her phone rings pulling at her attention interrupting her thoughts of Donnie. Before answering, she glances at the caller id. "Good morning, Mom."

"Good morning sweetheart. How are you feeling this morning?"

"I'm hanging in there".

"That's my girl. Has Donnie called?"

"No, he hasn't. Mom, I think my marriage is really over this time."

"Honey don't say that. You have to think positive about this. Donnie just needs some time to get his head together."

"Yeah some time to be with another woman. I know Brenda is filling his head with things that could truly destroy my marriage. Mom I confided in her about my marital problems and a lot more."

"Danielle, why would you do that?"

"I thought I could trust her."

"Danielle you could have come to me or one of your siblings to confide in."

"Mom, I couldn't have. I know how you guys feel about Donnie. He is like a biological son to you."

"What does that have to do with anything? You are my blood?"

"I almost had an affair with one of my co-workers. I know how you guys would have reacted if I had come and told you."

"Oh Dan you should know better than to confide in another woman and you should have not allowed her to move in with you and your family. You can trust very few women around your husband. I thought I taught you better than that."

"I know mom. I'm sorry I let this happen."

"Danielle you did nothing wrong. You said you thought about having an affair but you didn't. Donnie was the one who cheated."

"Why don't you and the boys spend the night with me tonight? We can get the boys up early and go Christmas shopping?"

"I don't know mom, I'll see."

"Well, I just called to check on you. I told your brothers and sister what has happen after you guys left last night."

"What did Jordan have to say?"

"Oh you know Jordan. He could ring Donnie's neck. Mark and Matthew were upset about it too. Richard and Sonny both said they thought Brenda was a conniving witch."

"I guess everyone could see that but me, but I have learned a valuable lesson through all of this".

"Are the boys up yet?"

"No they are still asleep."

"What time are you guys coming?"

"We should be there around three. I want to be there when Jasmine arrives."

"Okay baby, I'll see you guys then."

Danielle continues to lay after she hangs up with her mother. The house is too quiet. The silence suddenly feels like a knife through her heart. A wave of panic suddenly consumes her. She feels in her heart that her marriage is truly over.

~ C ~

As Danielle lays there thinking, she hears the sound of tiny feet echoing softly on the hardware floor and all at once two bodies lunge into her bed.

"Good morning Mommy," the boys say in unison.

"Good morning boys."

"Mommy is daddy ever coming back?" Derek, her youngest son asks.

"Daddy doesn't love us anymore does he Mommy?" Donnie Jr. asks.

Danielle's heart aches for the boys as reality sets in that they are the ones who are affected by their parents' actions.

"No sweetheart, your dad loves you boys very much."

"Then why doesn't he come home?" Her oldest ask.

"He will just give your dad sometime to get himself together. Right now, your dad is very busy and has a lot on his mind. Are you boys ready for breakfast?" Danielle asks as he hops out of bed.

"Yes," Derek yells as Donnie Jr. follows along in silence.

Jordan sits at his kitchen table drinking his morning coffee. He has been counting down the hours until he will finally see Jasmine again.

Jordan has spent the last two nights lying awake in bed thinking of her. It has been five long years since he last seen her and then, he only got a glimpse of her when she came to visit her parents.

He remembers the day she got married as if it was yesterday. He was devastated that he let her get away. He made a promise to himself that if he ever got another chance to be with her, she would be his forever.

The morning went by quickly for Danielle. She just finished her potato salad, greens and a peanut butter cake. She has less than an hour to get herself and the boys ready in order to arrive at her mom's on time. She wants to be there to see the look on Jordan's face when Jasmine arrives.

Jordan arrives at his mom's at exactly two thirty. His brothers and sisters and their families are already there.

As he enters the house, the smell of turkey and baked ham consumes him. He walks into the kitchen where he finds his mom working away. He put his finger up to his mouth motioning for his sisters to stay quiet. Jordan sneaks up behind his mom and wraps his arms around her. "Happy Thanksgiving Mom."

Mrs. Daniels jumps, "Jordan you are going to give me a heart attack." Jordan laughs as he plants a kiss on his mom's cheek.

"What are you doing sneaking up on an old woman like me?"

"I'm sorry Mom; I just get a kick out of getting you all riled up.

"Do you ladies need my help with anything?"

"Yes, you can take that turkey and ham out of the oven for me." Jordan removes his jacket and hangs it on the coat rack. He removes the turkey and ham out of the oven and places them on top of the kitchen stove.

"Is there anything else I can do?"

"No, darling we have everything under control."

Jordan was on his way to join his brothers in the family room when the doorbell rings.

"I'll get it," Jordan yells. Jordan opens the door to find Ronnie and his family.

"Happy Thanksgiving", Jordan says as he kisses Sheila on the cheek. He then turns to his two beautiful goddaughters and grabs them both up in his arms and kiss them on their cheeks.

"I can't believe how big you girls have gotten. Pretty soon I won't be able to hold the both of you at the same time. You girls are looking more like your dad everyday what a curse."

"You know that's a blessing that they got their looks from their dad."

Sheila looks at her husband and shakes her head.

"Where's your mom, Jordan?"

"She is in the kitchen with the rest of the hens."

Sheila makes her way to the kitchen with the rest of the women while Ronnie and Jordan walk back to the family room to watch the football game with his brothers.

Denise Hill

CHAPTER 12

It is three o'clock and everyone has arrived at the Daniels except for Jasmine. Jordan is anxious. He tries to get into the game but his mind is somewhere else and the men know it. Jordan continues to sit ignoring the comments about his favorite team who is now down by 14 points.

Ten minutes later, the doorbell rings again interrupting Jordan's thoughts. Matthew who is sitting by the window gets a glimpse of Vanessa standing at the door. Jordan cannot move his heart begins to accelerate until he hears her voice.

"Vanessa, what the hell is she doing here?"

Matthew burst out laughing.

"Man this is not funny."

"Yes it is, this is going to be an interesting day, nothing but drama," Ronnie says.

Jordan hops up out of his chair and is in the living room in record time.

"Happy Thanksgiving, Jordan," Vanessa says as she walks up to hug Jordan.

Mrs. Daniels can tell Jordan is not happy to see Vanessa so she decides to leave the two alone.

~ cvi ~

"Vanessa what the hell are you doing here?" The cold tone in Jordan's voice is back. This was the second time he has spoken to her with such hate.

"Did you forget that your mother invited me three weeks ago?"

"Oh, and so you decided to come even though we are no longer together."

"Jordan I miss you. I want things to be the way they used to be," Vanessa says as she reaches up to touch Jordan's face.

Jordan turns his head and takes a step back.

"Vanessa if you have come to try and win me back you are wasting your time. I suggest you uninvited yourself and leave."

"No, I am not going anywhere. Your mom invited me so I am staying."

"Alright, suit yourself, but don't start acting like we are a couple because we are not. I cannot believe you showed up. What do you have up your sleeves, Vanessa?"

"Nothing Jordan, I want you to see that we belong together."

"Oh my god, you have really lost your mind. Do you honestly think I would get back with someone who has done to me what you have done? Do you honestly believe that? I suggest you move on because I have."

"Who is she Jordan?"

"Vanessa, I would really appreciate it if you would leave and let me enjoy this day with my family."

"I am your family too. I know you broke off our engagement, but I know you only did this because you are hurt."

"Hurt, don't you dare touch me", Jordan shouts as he moves Vanessa's hand away.

Mrs. Daniels and the women listened to the heated words pass between Jordan and Vanessa.

Mrs. Daniels feels bad. She completely forgot about inviting Vanessa when she invited Jasmine.

"We are not having any of this," Mrs. Daniels says as she walks out of the kitchen into the living room. Now you two stop all that nonsense. This is a day to be thankful. I will not allow Satan to ruin this day. What is done is done. Let's just make the best of it." Mrs. Daniels leads Vanessa into the kitchen with the other women. Jordan walks over to the window and holds his head down. He could not believe Vanessa had the balls to show up today. If it were not for his mom, he would have thrown her ass out. He knows Vanessa is only there to see if he had brought a date.

Jasmine pulls up in front of the Daniels. She can tell by the cars that she is the last one to arrive.

Jasmine's heart begins to beat rapidly, the way it always does whenever she thinks about Jordan. A mixture of relief and anticipation soars through her realizing that she is about to embark upon a phase of her life that she has been looking forward to for a long time.

As she strides nervously up the walkway she remembers all the good times she and Danielle shared in this house. This was like a second home to her. She spent more time here than she did at her own home partly because she had a big crush on Jordan.

Jasmine was so excited when Mrs. Daniels had called to invite her over. She thought this would be a perfect opportunity for her to see Jordan again. Jasmine had thought about Jordan over the years and had even compared him to her husband but her husband could never match up to Jordan.

Just as Jordan was about to return to the family room, he looks up just in time to see Jasmine walking up the walkway.

Jasmines hand is poised to ring the doorbell when the front door opens. Jasmine looks up into his face and for a moment, her heart flipped crazily.

Jordan feels as though his heart has dropped to his stomach as he lays eyes on the prettiest face and smile that has occupied a place in his heart for years.

The entire house goes silent. You can hear a pin drop and everyone's eyes are glued to Jordan and Jasmine.

Vanessa purposely walks into the living room where she sees the curious stares as she notices Jordan and a woman standing at the front door.

The two stand there an unspoken understanding pass between them. On impulse, Jordan leans forward and kisses her on the lips. Jasmine thought she would lose it. The two stand there in silence until Matthew walks up.

"Don't' just stand there Jordan. Let her in out of the cold," Matthew says as he walks up to Jasmine and leads her inside the house. "You will have to excuse my brother's manners today."

Everyone greets Jasmine and goes back to doing what they were doing. Vanessa stands and watches the two exchange looks of desire. She notices how Jordan struggles to maintain some self-control. This is the reason Jordan broke off our engagement, she thinks.

Vanessa walks toward them clearing her throat causing the two to turn in her direction.

"Jasmine this is Vanessa. Vanessa this is someone who has been a part of our family for years. She is also Danielle's best friend. I have known Jasmine since

~ CX ~

she was a little snot nose girl. Her and Danielle use to follow me around all the time." Jasmine playfully punches Jordan in the arm.

"Hi, it's a pleasure to meet you," Jasmine says.

Vanessa gives Jasmine a fake smile and pulls Jordan to her.

"I need to speak with you in private."

Jasmine makes her way to the kitchen where the women have been working quietly hoping and praying that Vanessa does not cause any drama.

"Jasmine do you remember Ronnie's wife Sheila?" Mrs. Daniels asks as she points to Sheila.

"Yes, I do. How have you been Sheila?"

"Oh, I have been doing fine and yourself."

"Things are better." As Jasmine smiles.

"I bet." Monica says smiling at Jasmine.

"And what is that supposed to mean Mrs. Monica?"

"Girl, you and I both know you and Jordan still have the hot's for each other. Everyone can see it. Now the both of you are single, look out now."

Everyone in the kitchen bursts out laughing.

"I know that's right." Theresa says Jordan's eldest sister.

Jasmine walks over to where Danielle stands and whispers into her ear, "Have you heard from Donnie?"

"No and I probably won't."

"Don't think like that Dan, you guys have been together too long to let some tramp break up your marriage." Jasmine tells Danielle as she hugs her.

"Tell me about it."

"Have you tried calling him?"

"No I haven't. You know I thought he would call me by now but I guess he is too busy having fun with you know who."

"It's hard to believe that he hasn't even called the boys. Speaking of the boys, where are they?"

"They're in the family room with the men."

"Let me go in there and see my boys."

Jasmine and Vanessa pass each other as Vanessa makes her way back to the kitchen.

Before Jasmine can get to the family room, Jordan comes up from behind and wraps his arms around her. Jordan is losing control and he cannot help himself. He pulls her into his mom's guest bedroom and closes the door behind them and backs her up against the wall. Jordan can feel Jasmines body trembling. He runs his finger across her face as he looks at her dark brown skin gleaming in the sunlight that shines through the window.

"Are you nervous Jasmine?"

"Nervous, nervous does not come close to what I am feeling right now."

"Tell me, what you are feeling?"

"My goodness Jordan. Why are you putting me on the spot and why are you smiling at me like that?"

"You are more beautiful than I imagined. I love the way your eyes light up when you talk and that smile, man it drives me crazy."

Jordan gently brushes his lips across her mouth allowing his lips to linger lightly against hers. Jasmine inhales drawing the scent of him in her nostrils. Jordan inhales deeply filling his lungs with oxygen. He knows this is not where he wants this to go this soon. A knock at the door interrupts what was about to happen between the two.

Michael sticks his head in grinning from ear to ear. "It's time for dinner you two."

Thankful for the interruption, Jasmine follows Michael into the dining room where everyone is already seated.

Embarrassed to say the least, she takes a seat across from Vanessa, which she later regrets. Jordan takes the only available seat, which is next to Vanessa.

Mrs. Daniels sits at the head of the table. She loves this time of the year when she has all of her kids together under one roof. It is just like the old days when the house was filled with joy and laughter. Nevertheless, this time of the year makes her really miss Jordan Sr. Jordan Sr. was a loving and devoted husband and father. His spirits were always high even when he was on his deathbed. It was hard at first for her to let go, but the kids were there to help her get through it, especially Jordan being the oldest. Jordan stepped up to the plate and took on a part time job working after school to help make ends meet but they did not always meet. There was one thing that the Daniels family had plenty of and that was love, and they had each other.

"Jordan, would you mind saying grace?"

"No not at all."

"Make it short and simple Jordan. You know how you can get carried away," Theresa said.

"Father, I want to thank you for allowing us to spend another day of Thanksgiving with our loved ones. Father I ask that you bless the hands that have prepared this wonderful meal and I hope it tastes as good as it smells. Amen."

"Jordan," Mrs. Daniels calls out.

"Mom you have your daughter to thank for that one. She said short and simple." Everyone at the dinner table laughs.

CHAPTER 13

"How was your trip Jasmine," Danielle asks?

"It was very productive," Jasmine says with a smile. She did not elaborate on the fact that she had to go back to Florida to finalize her divorce.

"Jasmine, I am going to cut to the chase with you. Is there something going on between Jordan and you?" Vanessa asks.

Stunned that Vanessa would come right out and ask her this question in front of everyone, Jasmine could only answer as truthful as she could.

"Jordan and I are friends. I have known Jordan practically all my life and since we're cutting to the chase, is there something going on between you and Jordan?"

Jordan smiles. He loves a woman who can hold her own.

Jordan sits back in his chair and waits for a response from Vanessa. He cannot wait to hear what she has to say.

"Jordan and I were engaged until a few days ago, but we're working on things right now."

Not liking her response Jasmine wants her to know that she knows Jordan and her are no longer together just friends. Now Vanessa has no idea that Danielle has already filled her in on what was going on with the two.

"So basically what you're saying is that you guys are just friends and that Jordan is free to date anyone he chooses. I will have to say though, the next woman he dates will surely appreciate him and treat him the way a good man should be treated," Jasmine replies.

Jasmine is shocked in herself. She did not know where this was coming from because she has never been so out spoken.

Vanessa was about to reply when Monica decides to direct the conversation into a different direction before it gets out of hand.

"Jasmine, have you been successful in finding a job?" Monica asks.

"No, I am still looking but I am sure something will fall through for me."

"Oh are you jobless," Vanessa asks with a smirk on her face.

"Yes, the company that I worked for in Florida was bought out and they brought in their own people. I received a hefty severance pay which will last me a little over a year. So I may be jobless, but I'm not broke."

"What type of job are you looking for Jasmine?" Jordan asks.

"I prefer something in business communications or marketing."

"Why don't you stop by my office on Monday morning? I have the perfect job for you if you're interested. It's not in business communications or marketing, but

I bet you will like it. I am on vacation next week but I could come into the office to discuss the job in greater details and so you can look around to see if the job is something that interests you."

"That sounds good to me. I would have never dreamed of working for the man that I had the biggest childhood crush on. What time should I be there?"

"Is nine o'clock too early?"

"No, that's perfect I'm an early riser."

"I just bet you are," Vanessa says.

"What is that supposed to mean, Vanessa?"

"Oh nothing, I'm just thinking out loud."

Jasmine gives Vanessa a look that says, "Don't fuck with me bitch." When it comes to Jordan Jasmine can be a bad and devious bitch.

Vanessa could have shot through the roof.

"Jordan I didn't know you had an open position." Vanessa says.

"I don't but I can create a position whenever I want and besides, there are plenty of things that she could do, if she chooses."

Jasmine steals a glance at Jordan and when their eyes collided for a heart stopping moment, he is telling her what words cannot.

Matthew and Michael both sit back in their chairs and watch with amusement while the episode plays out between Jordan, Jasmine and Vanessa, loving every bit of it. They both feel that it is time for their older brother to find that special someone and settle down. They know that person is Jasmine.

While everyone seem to be so concern about Jasmine and her well-being, Vanessa feels out of place and out done. She decides it is best that she leave. She does not want to be where she is not wanted. She only stopped by to spy on Jordan to see if he brought a date. Vanessa has what she needs so it is time for her to leave and rejoin her own family. She now knows why Jordan called off their engagement, but Jordan has a rude awakening if he thinks he can get rid of her this easy, he has another thing coming." I will wear Jasmine down to the point that she will cringe when she even hears the name Jordan."

After dinner, the women remain in the kitchen. They prepare plates to take home and make sure everything is put away.

Vanessa gets her coat and purse and she thanks Mrs. Daniels for the dinner. She was getting ready to leave when Jordan walks in to the kitchen.

"Jordan, can you walk me out to my car?"

Jordan looks at Vanessa. He knows she is going to try to start an argument about Jasmine but he will be ready for whatever she brings his way.

~ CXX ~

As soon as Jordan steps out the front door, Vanessa lets him have it.

"How dare you do this to me Jordan! We have only been broken up for three days and already you're seeing that bitch Jasmine."

"Wait a minute. Let's leave Jasmine out of this okay. I do not appreciate you calling her out of her name. You know nothing about her. Jasmine is a very nice and sweet woman. She is more of a woman than you will ever be. In case you forgot, I am free to date anyone I chose to so you have no right to question me about anyone. I am not dating Jasmine or anyone else now but if I chose to date Jasmine, that will be our business not yours. So I suggest you go and get with Thomas, the man you cheated on me with."

Jordan turns and opens the door and walks back into the house leaving Vanessa standing. "This is not the last of this Jordan, you better believe it", Vanessa yells out.

Monica, Loretta and Danielle linger in the kitchen talking after the rest of the family gathered into the family room when Matthew walks in.

"I'm not trying to be a matchmaker, but it is obvious that Jordan and Jasmine still have feelings for each other." Matthew says as he wraps his arms around his wife Monica.

"I know, I was observing the two of them and anyone can see that. I think that's why Vanessa took off," Danielle says.

"Man, I thought I would die when Vanessa asked Jasmine what she was to Jordan", Matthew said as he laughs loudly.

"I know she has got some nerve," Loretta replies.

"Hey Dan, have you heard from that husband of yours?" Her brother asks.

"No, I haven't."

"What is up with him?"

"Your guess is as good as mine."

It was Thanksgiving evening and Donnie is without his family, instead he is in a hotel with Brenda, the woman who helped destroy his marriage. He wonders how his boys are holding up, most of all he wonders how Danielle is doing. He wants so badly to be with them, especially today. He thought about calling but he knows it was no chance in hell that Danielle will let the boys speak with him. Against his better judgment, Donnie picks up the phone and dials his mother- in- law's number. He feels he will have a better chance to speak with his boys while she is there than if she was at home.

The phone rings three times before Matthew picks up. Donnie is just about to hang up when Matthew answers.

"Hey Matthew, is Danielle around?"

"Yeah, hold on."

Matthew hands Danielle the phone as he rest his body against the counter. He stands quietly as he watches his sister speak to her husband.

"How are you Danielle?"

"I'm okay."

"How are the boys doing?"

"They want to know why their daddy left and hasn't bothered to call them in seven days. They are also wondering if their dad doesn't love them anymore."

"Dan, I am sorry, you know that is not the case. I love you and my boys dearly."

"Yeah, you love me so much that you slept with another woman in our bed."

"Danielle I did not call you to argue with you about this. It's not what you think."

"It's not what I think. No, it's what I saw. Donnie, do you think I am stupid?"

"No, Danielle, I do not think you're stupid. Can I come and get the boys tomorrow around three and when I drop them off can we sit down and talk?"

"I guess."

"Tell my boys that I love them and that I will be there tomorrow at three. I love you Danielle."

As soon as Danielle hangs up the phone, the three that remained in the kitchen are all ears.

"What did he have to say?" Matthew asks.

"He wants to pick the boys up tomorrow and when he drops them off he wants to sit down and talk. He has the nerve to tell me it's not what I think."

"What kind of shit is he on?" Matthew asks.

Denise Hill

CHAPTER 14

Michael and Jordan find Matthew in the kitchen lollygagging. "Hey man, we need your help in the attic," Jordan says.

Another one of the Daniels family tradition was to put up the Christmas tree on Thanksgiving evening. The men went up to the attic to gather the Christmas tree and all the decorations. The kids love helping to decorate the tree. Each child had its own special ornament that each one places on the tree.

The family room was lively to say the least. Music plays as the men finish putting up the tree. The children wait patiently so that they can help decorate while the women sit around the fireplace talking and drinking hot chocolate while others drink coffee. The men of course have the hard stuff.

Jordan pours himself a glass of Hennessey and moves to the corner of the room.

He studies Jasmine from across the room as she talks with his mom and sisters.

Jordan could have kicked himself for losing control the way he had done earlier with Jasmine, but there was something about her, that made him lose it. Everytime he looks at her, he remembers their first kiss and how they both wanted it to continue. Yet as much as he desires her, he has reservations. He wonders about her marriage. What caused it to end, was she unfaithful, did she want kids because he did. That was one of his concerns with Vanessa. She said she wanted kids but he found out that she was secretly taking the pill.

Jasmine looks up and her eyes met Jordan in surprise. She smiles and it puts him over the edge. He motions for her to come to him.

Easing up from the couch, she walks over to the corner of the room where he stands.

"Are you enjoying yourself," he asks.

"Yes I am. How about you?"

"I always enjoy myself when I am around my loved ones. So I hear you've been out of town for a couple of days."

"Yes I had to go back to Florida to tie up some lose ends."

Jasmine walked out of court a free woman after several years of verbal and physical abuse that caused her to lose her unborn child. She lived the last three years of her life in hell and to find out that her ex-husband had another family that lived two streets from where they lived was the breaking point for her. She will never allow herself to be made a fool of over a man, once was more than enough to last her a lifetime.

"How long have you been divorced?"

"My divorce was final yesterday."

"Was that your decision or his?"

"Oh it was definitely my decision."

There was something in the way Jordan starred at her that sent a warm sensation down her spine. He was a man of elegance to say the least. Those eyes the color of honey and that dark chocolate skin would make any women beg him to take her.

"So tell me Mr. Daniels, what caused you to break off your engagement with Vanessa?"

"There were several things that made me break it off with her. You see Jasmine, the woman that I chose to marry has to have the same values that I have. I cannot and will not tolerate a cheater or a liar. Vanessa is a good woman but right now she doesn't know who she wants and I do not have the time to wait around until she finds out."

"I understand I lived with the lying and cheating for several years until I couldn't take it anymore. I tried so hard to make my marriage work but I couldn't make it work by myself."

"Was your ex ever abusive?"

Jasmine looked away as she thought about what she had experienced in her marriage. The pain was still there. "Jordan I rather not talk about my ex. He's in my past and that's where I want him to stay."

"I sorry Jasmine, I didn't mean to pry into your past." "That's okay, that's something that I will have to overcome. My parents think it is a good idea for me to talk about it so that I will always remember it and never allow myself to get in that predicament again, but right now, the wounds are still fresh."

An hour later, Jordan and Jasmine rejoins the family as they talk about their childhood. Jordan tells stories of how he would sneak girls into his room while his mom slept. "And all this time I thought I had the perfect sons", Mrs. Daniels says.

"Mom they did things that we would never do," Savannah said.

"I can vouch for that," Jasmine says.

"Oh listen to miss goody two shoes," Michael said.

"I wasn't a goody two shoe, I did my dirt as well."

"Yeah like what?" Mathew asked. Jasmine laughs, "I will never tell."

"I remember one time Danielle and I were walking one night and these guys stopped and asked us if we wanted to go to their house for drinks and we said yes and hopped in the car. We went to their house and had a couple of beers while they got high. Now that I think about it that was dangerous. They could have done anything to us, but they didn't. They were the perfect men. After we finished our drinks, they dropped us back off where they picked us up."

"I told you she was a goody two shoe. She only went because of Danielle." Everyone in the room laughs.

"Yeah Danielle was a bad influence", Theresa said.

"You have got a lot of nerves", Danielle chimes in. At least I did not sneak out of the house every night to go to Sonny's while his dad was at work. What did you guys do, watch television."

"Hey you leave me out of it", Sonny says.

"What about Richard and Savannah don't leave them out, Danielle says.

"Don't start Danielle, I will tell everything about you and Donnie," Savannah threatens.

"Oh what about Jasmine she was so in love with Jordan that she didn't have time for any boys." Theresa pulls a sheet of paper from her purse. "Let's see this is about twenty years old. Dear Jordan I love you with all my heart I want to have all your kids and be your wife, Love Jasmine."

"Oh my God, where did you find that?" Jasmine asks as she blushes from embarrassment.

"Well, since we are bringing things up, Jasmine, did you know that Jordan moped around here for months after you got married?" Ronnie asked.

"Jasmine, don't believe anything that comes out of this man's mouth," Jordan says.

~ CXXX ~

"You guys are a mess and to think all of this was going on right under my nose," Mrs. Daniels says.

At 9:30 P.M. everything was quiet at the Daniels resident, everyone has left except for Jordan and Jasmine. They continue to linger after the others departure, neither one wants to call it a night.

"Well, I guess I should say goodnight," Jasmine says as she reaches for her coat.

"Yeah, it's time for me to get home too. Let me walk you out to your car."

The two walk in silence, when they reach her car a smile touches his lips as he pulls Jasmine to him. He holds her in his arms. She looks up to see eyes that burn with want. Jordan lowers his head and brushes her lips with his own. Her lips part as his tongue enters her mouth. He deepens the kiss, for short period of time their tongues dance a dance of desire. Jordan removes his lips from her mouth as he kiss her eyes her ears her neck and her throat then without warning, he backs away from her. "Good night Jasmine," he says as he opens the car door for her. Jasmine smiles a weak smile, the edges of her mouth barely binding upward.

"Good night Jordan."

Jasmine drives away in frustration. It was as if Jordan was rejecting her again, as he had done fifteen years ago.

CHAPTER 15

The next morning Jasmine wakes early as usually. She showers, dresses, and was out the door in no time. She decides this was the best time to get a little Christmas shopping done.

After shopping, Jasmine decides to pay a visit to Jordan. She looks over the directions that Danielle had given her and proceeds to drive. Slowing at a section where the street divides into four directions, Jasmine glances at the directions again. She follows the sign pointing the way to Jordan's home. It is a secluded area, that contained large homes, if not for the directions, she would have sworn she was in the wrong neighborhood. "I didn't know Jordan had it going on like this," she says to herself.

Jasmine spots Jordan's Mercedes in the driveway and maneuvers her SUV in front of his house. She turns the engine off and sits there.

She remembers Danielle telling her that if she ever wanted to be with him, she would have to do everything possible to breakdown the barrier that he has up.

The sun was rising when Jordan woke. He looks at the clock on the nightstand, it is a little after eight. He sits up swing he legs over the side of the bed. He decides he would make a visit to Danielle's to see how she and the boys are doing.

Jordan staggers into the bathroom. He brushes his teeth, shaves and heads for the shower. He had another restless night. He had tossed and turned all night thinking of Jasmine.

The weather was sunny and mild for the late November morning. Jasmine takes a moment and closes her eyes against the sunshine before heading up the walkway. As she walks up the walkway, she admires the solid oak door with the stained glass insets.

Before ringing the doorbell, she asks herself, "What am I doing here?"

Jordan had just finished showering when he hears the sound of the doorbell. He wonders who this could be at his door this early in the morning. Still dressed in his bath towel, he makes his way down the stairs.

Jordan opens the door half expecting to find Vanessa on his doorstep, but to his surprise there stands Jasmine.

Jordan stands with a puzzled look on his face. He would have expected anyone other than Jasmine. by the way

Jasmine stands there mesmerized by the way Jordan looks in nothing but his bath towel. He looks good enough to eat, Jasmine thought. His chest reminds her of a Hershey's chocolate bar. She wants to take a lick to see if it taste as good as it looks.

"I'm sorry to disturb you so early, were you busy?"

"No, come on in. I'm just surprised to see you."

"I got your address from Danielle, I hope you don't mind."

"No don't be silly." Jordan escorts Jasmine to the family room and takes her coat.

"Make yourself comfortable while I finish dressing." Jordan turns to leave and stops.

"Have you had breakfast?"

"No, I haven't. I left my apartment pretty early to get some Christmas shopping done."

"Would you like to go out for breakfast?"

"Sure, why not."

Jordan throws on a pair of blue jeans and a white polo sweater. He checks his appearance in the mirror before heading downstairs.

Jasmine has only seen one room of the house but what she sees is more than what she expected. She wonders why a single man with no children would have such a large home. The family room is large with a large stone fireplace; the cherry wood furniture gives the room a look of elegance. A baby grand piano sits at the far side of the room. Jasmine is puzzled she has never known Jordan to play the piano but maybe he learned over the years, she thinks. This room looks like something she has seen in a magazine. She wonders what the rest of the house looks like. Jasmine pictures herself sitting on the ledge looking out the bay window on a cold and raining day drinking coffee and reading a good book.

Jordan makes his way down the stairs as Jasmine waits patiently. Jordon stands in the entryway of the family room trying to get his emotions under control.

"Did I take too long?"

Jasmine turns to the sound of his voice. "I was beginning to wonder if I was going to have to come and look for you."

"I didn't take that long, did I?"

Jasmine smiles, "No, I'm just pulling your leg."

"Do you still want to go and have breakfast?"

"Yes, my stomach is growling."

Jordan laughs. "Okay, let's go. I wouldn't want you passing out on me."

"I see you're not going to let me live that down are you?"

"What are you talking about?" Jordan says with a serious face.

Years ago when Jasmine was in her late teens, Jordan had taken Danielle and Jasmine to his friend's farm in the country for a barbeque. Jordan's friend had several horses on his farm and ever since Jasmine was little, she has been fascinated with horses.

Jasmine could not tear herself away from the horses long enough to eat. It had been nine hours since she had eaten and her blood sugar level was low. She eventually passed out giving them a good scare. Jordan has never let her live that day down.

"You know what I am talking about, don't try and play dumb with me Mr."

"I see you have gotten to be a little feisty over the years".

"And why do you say that?"

"The Jasmine that I knew would have never shown up at someone's home without being invited."

"I'm sorry Jordan I can leave if it's a problem?"

"Oh no, don't get me wrong, Jasmine. I am talking about you in the past, as I remember you were very shy except for one other time I have never seen you be aggressive. Like yesterday with Vanessa. You held your ground with her and I like that. Jasmine believe it or not, I am glad you are here." Jordan moves closer to Jasmine, his heart beating rapidly. He touches the side of her face with his hand bringing her face upward to look directly into his eyes. "When I feel the time is right, I will let you in on a little secret," he says as he brushes his lips against hers.

Jasmine is a little confused to say the least. She went from feeling as if she had been an intrusion to feeling as though Jordan felt for her what she has always felt for him.

"Now let's get out of here so that I can feed you," he says as he grabs her hand and leads her to the front entryway.

The two ride in silence until Jordan notices Vanessa trailing behind them in his rearview mirror.

"I can't believe her," Jordan says.

"Believe who?"

"Vanessa is following behind us," Jasmine turns to look and shakes her head.

"She is going to be a thorn in my side," Jordan says.

"She doesn't have to be Jordan. You need to make her understand that it is over between the two of you."

"Right, but you don't know Vanessa like I do."

Jordan and Jasmine arrive at Perkins restaurant. He pulls into a parking spot and Vanessa pulls in right beside them. Jordan gets out of the car, walks around to the passenger side, and opens the door for Jasmine. The two walk to the entrance of the restaurant before they enter Vanessa get out of her car.

"Jordan, I need to speak with you for a minute," she yells.

"Vanessa what is it, I don't have time for any of your games and I don't appreciate you following me around."

"It's okay Jordan, go ahead, talk with her, and get it over," Jasmine says.

"No, I refuse to speak with her. If she needed to talk she should have called, but no she choose to follow me. I am not putting up with that shit."

Jordan and Jasmine continue to make their way into the restaurant while Vanessa stands outside.

Jordan and Jasmine stand inside the restaurant waiting for the host to escort them to their table.

"How many in your party?" The host asks.

"It's just the two of us. Is there any way we can have a table close to the back?"

"I'll see what I can do," the host says as he walks back to find a table for them.

A minute later, the host came back, "You two can follow me."

As they follow the host, Jasmine notices some of the single women giving Jordan the eye but he continues to walk as he holds her hand as though they don't exist. This would not have been the case with her ex-husband. He would have smile and said hello, on occasions Jasmine even caught him winking at some of the women. He had been very disrespectful, especially in public.

When they arrive at their table, Jordan pulls out her chair and waits until she takes her seat before he takes his. What a gentlemen she thinks. This is something that she is not used to. Her ex-husband Ricky was her one and only boyfriend. Now when she looks back to their first date, it should have been their first and last date because she had to pay her own way to the movies and pay for her dinner afterwards. Nevertheless, she was young and wanted so badly to fall in love. She's a romantic at heart and since she could not have the love of her life, she settled for the next best thing. The one thing that she has learned from this is that when you settle you miss what God has for you and then you have to wait until your time comes around again.

Once they both were seated, the waiter comes out and takes their order. By this time, Jasmine's stomach has begun to growl.

Jordan looks up at her and laughs, "I see someone's really hungry."

"Yeah, I'm hungrier than I thought."

~ cxl ~

Denise Hill

CHAPTER 16

After Breakfast had concluded, Jordan and Jasmine orders coffee and continue to sit and talk. They talk about everything besides the reason the two are single. Jordan is curious as to why she ended her marriage and Jasmine was curious as to why he had broken off his engagement with Vanessa.

True enough Jasmine and Danielle had talked about Jordan and Vanessa but Danielle did not know why Jordan had broken off the engagement with Vanessa she had just assumed he broke it off when he learned that Jasmine had moved back.

Jordan asked questions about her marriage but Jasmine skirted around his questions so he decides to leave it alone. He figures when she is ready to talk about it she would.

Vanessa sits outside in her car waiting on Jordan and Jasmine to come out of the restaurant. She wants so badly to go inside and confront the two but she does not want to cause a scene. Vanessa continues to sit for the next twenty minutes before deciding to leave.

After they finish their coffee, Jordan pays the bill and the two head back to his place where they sit parked in his driveway while they continue to talk.

"Jordan, do you really think I am qualified for the assistant accounting manager position or are you doing this because you feel sorry for me?"

"First of all, I do not feel sorry for you in anyway. There is no reason for me to feel sorry for you and second, if I didn't think you could handle the position, I wouldn't have offered it to you. I know several people who I could call in a favor to get you a position somewhere else."

"I just wanted to be sure because I can't stand to have anyone feeling sorry for me. It's not like I am out on the street, besides I have my savings and my severance pay which should last me at least a year and a half."

"You won't have to touch your savings or your severance anymore because your salary will be eighty thousand a year plus a twenty percent annually bonus, that's if you decide to take the job."

"Are you serious?"

"Yes, I take good care of my employees. You will see."

Deciding that he wanted to see more of Jasmine he asks her out for dinner. "What time should I expect you?"

"I should be at your place around six maybe we could go somewhere afterwards."

"That sounds good to me."

Jordan walks Jasmine to her car and opens the door for her, but before she has a chance to move, Jordan pulls her to him. The nearness of him makes her giddy. A sudden flood of heat rushes through her as he looks down into her eyes. Jordan inhales her beauty. The heat that rushes overwhelms him from one end of his body to the other. He brushes his lips against hers. Her mouth opens allowing him to enter. His heart was beating heavily against her own. He is losing control. The rush of heat is suddenly too intoxicating for him so he pulls his mouth away from her and holds her tightly.

For several minutes, the two stand in the street embracing each other. Jordan leans down and kisses Jasmine on the forehead. "You better get going while you can."

Jasmine smiles as she eases out of his embrace. "I guess I'll see you at six," Jasmine says.

Jordan stands on the sidewalk and watches as Jasmine drives off. He could have kicks himself for losing control with her for a second time. Jordan is use to beautiful women, but there is something about Jasmine that causes him to think of hot sex every time he is near her.

Vanessa had decided against having Thanksgiving dinner with Jared and Jonathan but suggested lunch at her place today at one o'clock.

On the drive home, Vanessa has mixed emotions about their meeting. She only wishes that Jonathan and she could have met on better terms. She can tell that Jonathan has much animosity toward her. After thinking about the situation she realizes that he has every right to be angry but what she cannot understand is why he is taking it out on her, she has been in the dark just as he has.

Vanessa arrives home and checks her messages. She has a message from Jared confirming today's lunch. Vanessa phones Jared back but gets his voice mail. "Hey it's Vanessa. Lunch is still on. I want to get this over. Jared I would really appreciate it if you could arrive before Jonathan gets here. I will see you around 12:45."

Jared walks out of the bathroom as he hears Vanessa's voice. Jared had already planned to arrive a little early because of the way his conversation had gone with Jonathan. Jared had phoned Jonathan several days ago and their conversation had not gone well. He had been arrogant, condescending and had even tried being intimidating, but Jared is not a person who was easily intimidated.

Jared had phoned Jonathan two months ago and had explained to him about the will his aunt had found leaving Jonathan and Vanessa with equal controlling interest in Cole Laboratory. Their conversation had gone well. He seemed very understanding but now it seems as though Jonathan has a change of heart and a different attitude. It almost seems as though someone has been filling his head with negative thoughts. Jared knew of only one person who would do this,

Jonathan's aunt. She has had it in for Vanessa's mom for years and everyone that knows her knows it.

Vanessa had just finished freshening up when she hears the doorbell. Thinking it is Jared she rushes to the door opens it before looking through the peephole. When she opens the door, she gets the shock of her life. There stood Jonathan with a bouquet of fresh flowers. Vanessa stands there for a second stunned, "Oh I thought you were Jared," is all Vanessa can say.

Jonathon was all prepared to ask Vanessa to buy him out, but when he arrives, the feeling that comes over him is so overwhelming that he could not go through with his plan.

Jonathan hands Vanessa the flowers, "These are for you as a peace offering." Still stunned, Vanessa accepts the flowers and invites Jonathan in. Vanessa motions for him to take a seat on the coach.

"I'll take your coat just as soon as I get these flowers in some water."

Vanessa feels awkward about being there without Jared and wishes Jared would hurry up and get there.

Vanessa makes her way back to the living room, takes Jonathan's coat, and hangs it in the closet. She walks over takes a seat on the loveseat that is directly across from Jonathan.

~ cxlvi ~

"I'm sorry we had to meet this way," Vanessa says.

"I know I feel awful of accusing you and your mom of trying to keep the company from me."

"I had no idea that you even existed. I grew up wanting an older brother and to find out at the age of Thirty-two that I had one all this time. Did you know about me?"

"I found out about you the day you were born."

"Oh I see."

"I blamed my dad or should I say our dad for my Mom's death. She never stopped loving him and it tore her apart when he married. She was never the same after that."

"I'm sorry to hear that and I hope we can put that behind us because neither one of us had anything to do with what happened between our parents."

"It will take some time but I totally agree with you." Jonathan gets up from the couch makes his way over to Vanessa. She stands up and they two siblings embrace each other.

Jared stands in the entryway as he watches and listens to the two siblings. He had let himself in when he saw that Jonathan had already arrived. Jared was ready for a round with Jonathan if he had said anything to upset Vanessa but was glad to have witnessed the coming together of brother and sister. This has been a long time coming he thought.

Jared makes his way to the living room. "Hey, did I miss anything?" Jared asks.

"I thought I told you to be here at 12:45."

"I'm sorry, I tried but my lady friend didn't want to let me go."

"Whatever," Vanessa says.

Jared and Jonathan embrace each other, I'm sorry for being an ass the other day."

"You are right you were being an ass but apology accepted. Hey, is lunch ready? I am starved."

"Why didn't you tell that lady friend of yours to feed you?"

"Ha, ha very funny. If I didn't have to rush over here she would have done more than feed me."

Both men laugh.

Vanessa softly punched Jared in the arm, "TMI."

Lunch had gone well with the threesome. They sat for hours sharing their childhood days with Jonathan. They eventually moved to the family room after lunch where Vanessa pulls out her family photos. They laugh and joke with each

other about some of the pictures. All laughter came to a halt when Vanessa turns

the page that has a picture of Jonathan Sr. He looks so much like Jonathan Jr.

There was no mistake that he was his father's son. Jonathan thought his heart

would stop. He missed his dad so much especially while he was growing up.

He feels a pang of jealously roaring its ugly head out but he refuses to give in to it.

Vanessa looks up at Jonathan who has tears in his eyes. "I'm sorry," Jonathan

says as he wipes his eyes. I owe you two a big apology. I had every intention of

coming over here giving you people hell. You have done nothing but welcome me

warmly. I wanted to blame you so much Vanessa for my dad not being in my life

while I was growing up. When I turned 18, my mom sat me down and talked to me

about my dad. I found out that he had been paying child support through my aunt

Judy on a weekly basis to send to us because he had no knowledge of my

whereabouts and my mom wanted to keep it that way. My mom felt it was time for

me to make my own decision about my dad and I decided to keep him out of my

life out of anger for him and his family. I found out about you Vanessa when I

was twelve. I overheard my aunt Judy telling my mom that your mom had just

given birth to a baby girl that made me angrier because you would be getting all

my dad's love. After my mom died, I kept in contact with Aunt Judy while I was

in college on a weekly basis. She kept the hatred that I had for your family going

for all these years up until today. Today it stops. You are my blood and I want to

be a part of your life if you will allow me to be a part of it."

Vanessa and Jonathan sit there embracing each other with tears in their eyes. It was a touching moment for Jared.   He steps outside on the porch to get some air and to let brother and sister unite.

The tears began to roll down his face from the feeling he got bringing them together.

~ cl ~

Denise Hill

CHAPTER 17

Jordan makes his back to his car he has plans to stop by Danielle's to see how she and the boys were doing. He wanted to talk with her yesterday, but decided to wait until today.

"Hey Uncle Jordan," Donnie Jr. and Derek says as they raced to Jordan.

"How are my favorite nephews doing today?"

"We want our dad, Uncle Jordan but he doesn't live with us anymore. Isn't that right Mommy?" Derek asks.

"Hey boys why don't the two of you go to your room and watch television so that Uncle Jordan can talk with your mom."

"Okay Uncle Jordan," Derek says. Donnie Jr. follows behind his younger sibling. The separation has taken a toll on him more so that his brother. His dad and he have always been the closest and not being able to speak with his dad on a regular basis makes him feel as if he has done something wrong to cause his dad not to love them anymore.

Jordan walks over to the couch where Danielle sits and takes a seat next to her. "How are you holding up baby girl?"

"I' m hanging in there."

"Have you heard from Donnie?"

"He called yesterday while we were at moms. He wants to stop by today and get the boys and later this evening he wants to sit down and talk."

"That's good. The two of you need to think about the kids and how this will affect them if you can't work things out. Now I am not saying that what Donnie has done was right by no means but you are the one who brought this woman into your lives."

"I know I keep beating myself up over this. How could I have been so stupid?"

"You were not stupid. You tried to help a friend out and in the end she shit on you?" Danielle laughs.

"I'm serious, that is exactly what she did. You trusted her confided in and in return, she shit on you. That is my new definition for someone who you consider a friend who sleeps with your mate. Brenda did to you what Vanessa has done to me. You can sit here and dwell on it and let it eat you up inside or you can put it behind you and move on. That is what I have done. Don't get me wrong, I dwelled on it for a while until I decided that it was no longer worth it. It was a hard decision to make but I know I made the right choice. Now you have to make that decision with Donnie and yourself. You can forgive him and move on or you can end your marriage, which will have an impact on your boys."

"I know you're right but I am not the only one in this. Donnie has to want this also. What if he tells me that he wants a divorce?"

"Then you will have to do what you have to do and make the most of it. You know you will have your family's support no matter what the outcome is."

"Yeah, I know."

Jordan and Danielle were still talking when Donnie knocks at the door. It feels strange for Donnie to knock at his own front door. He was not accustomed to being without his wife and kids if only he could go back in time and change things.

Jordan walks to the door to let Donnie in while Danielle goes to the boys' bedroom to get them ready.

"What's up Jordan?" Donnie says.

"Hey Donnie," is all Jordan could say. He is angry with Donnie for putting his sister and the boys through this.

"Jordan I know you don't think much of me right now, but it is not what you think. I am still trying to figure this out myself."

"It's not about what I think it should be about your family and how this has affected them. You need to make this right man." Jordan sticks his head out the door he thought he had seen a passenger in Donnie's car.

~ cliv ~

"Man I can't believe you. You have the nerve to come over here with Brenda in your car and you say it is not what I think. You are a poor excuse for a man," Jordan says as he makes his way back to the boys' bedroom.

"Before you go out there, I want you to know that Brenda is out there in the car."

"What, you have got to be kidding me." Danielle storms out of the boy's bedroom and into the family room where Donnie stands.

"How could you be so fucking stupid by bringing that bitch with you? I don't want her around my boys."

"Danielle, don't do this, I miss my boys and I am still their father I have every right to see them."

"Right now I say what your rights are and right now you have the right to walk the fuck out of here."

Jordan was still in the room with the boys and had closed their door so they would not witness their parents going at each other.

"Mom is not going to let us go with dad, is she?" Donnie Jr. asks.

"I don't know DJ, there are things that your parents have to work out before you guys can become a family again."

"Did we do something wrong Uncle Jordan?" Donnie asks.

"No, and don't you ever think that. This is between your mom and your dad. Right now they don't see eye to eye on some things so they have to work it out. You two stay right here, I will be right back."

Jordan wants to make sure things do not get out of hand between Donnie and Danielle.

By the time, Jordan makes it back to the family room Danielle and Donnie are going at each other.

Danielle was in tears. She had been ready to take Donnie back and make things work for her family but after seeing Brenda in the car, changed everything.

"Hey you guys need to keep it down. The boys do not need to hear their parents carrying on like this."

"Danielle, go ahead and let the boys go so that they can spend some time with their dad. The kids have not done anything, so don't punish them, but I will say one thing, Donnie you are wrong to bring Brenda with you. You have not shown my sister any respect. I will not sit around and let you continue to disrespect her. I thought you were better than that."

"I need to go out there and beat her ass like I wanted to do when I caught that bitch in my bed."

~ clvi ~

"No Danielle, that's not going to solve anything. You need to deal with your husband he is the one who brought her over here."

Danielle glances at Donnie and she sees the sadness and disappointment in his eyes. He has always respected and looked up to Jordan and when Jordan called him on his actions, his eyes shows what he feels.

The boys run out to greet their dad. Donnie let the tears flow. His boys were his life. He was hurt that he has to live apart from them. At that moment, Donnie knows he has to make things right with Danielle so that he can have his family back.

Donnie drops Brenda off at her mom's. He told her earlier what his intentions were with Danielle and that she can no longer share his hotel room.

Donnie takes the boys to McDonald's for dinner and they catch a movie afterwards. He enjoys seeing his boys and seeing them laugh. He miss hearing their voices whether they were fighting with each other or just being boys. He dreads having to take them back and having to go to his hotel room alone but most of all, his misses his wife. Things were not always rocky with them. Most of their marriage was good and he wants to get things back to that point.

Later that evening, Donnie pulls into the driveway. "Dad will you be coming home with us?" Derek asks.

"No, not today son, I will be back home soon, I promise. I want you boys to know that my being away has nothing to do with my love for you because I will always love the two of you and your mom."

Donnie walks the boys to the door. It tears him up inside when he bends down to hug them and they refuse to let him go. The boys begin to cry which brings tears to his eyes.

Danielle stands in the doorway watching with tears in her eyes; it breaks her heart to see her boys in tears because of their parents' actions.

"Come on boys, your dad can come back and get you another time."

"Danielle, we have got to talk, this is tearing me up not being able to tuck my boys in at night."

"Well Donnie that is something that you should have thought about before you did what you did."

"Danielle how long are you going to punish me for this? Why can't we sit down and talk like mature adults. I know you are hurt and angry you have every right to be. I am hurting too, but what is worst is that we are hurting the boys. Can't you try and think of someone else's feeling for a change?"

"Donnie you go to hell," Danielle says as she closes the door in his face.

~ clviii ~

Denise Hill

CHAPTER 18

Jordan climbs the stairs to the fourth floor and enters his bedroom. He kicks his shoes off and lies across the bed. He has mixed emotions about his dinner date with Jasmine. He had enjoyed her company today and if he was honest with himself, he did not want it to end. There was no doubt in his mind that he could fall head over heels in love with her. That is what frightens him. He wants to take his time with her. There are things that he needs to work out with himself. There comes a time in a person's life where you have to examine yourself and figure out why you constantly keep going through relationships after relationships that all end the same way. He wants to find out what he is doing or not doing that cause the women that he had loved to cheat.

Jordan knows that Jasmine has been through a rough marriage but he did not know the details. The last thing that he wants to do is cause her more pain.

Jasmine has spent more than two hours trying to find the perfect outfit. She wants to look sexy but not provocative. She has been through half the clothes in her closest before deciding on a brown fitted suede dress. Jasmine pulls a box from her closet that contains a new pair of brown suede boots that she had purchased before leaving Florida.

~ clx ~

Jasmine was excited to say the least. For so many years, she has dreamed of this day, a day that Jordan and she would actually go on a real date. She can only hope that this was the beginning of something special.

However, today, Jordan has been a little distant toward her he did not seem like the person who she had shared a passionate kiss with at his moms.

Jasmine glanced at the clock she has a little over an hour before Jordan will arrive. She makes her way to the bathroom. She runs her a bubble bath and places her IPod in her Bose speaker. She goes to her light jazz play list. She lit several candles as she has always done while taking a bath. This always seems to relax and ease her mind.

By the time Jasmine finish dressing, it is 5:55 p.m. She stands in front of the mirror to observe herself. The image stares back at her, she turns all the way around staring at herself admiring the way her body fills out her dress.

Jordan lay across his bed and has fallen into a deep sleep. While vision of Jasmine invades his dreams like so many of his dreams, Jasmine has come to him and they make love but this time it is different. He has always been the one in control, but this time Jasmine is in control. She slowly walks over to him as she removes the scarf that is around her neck. She begins to tie his hands together. Once his hands are tied, she reaches behind her, pulls out a switchblade, and proceeds to slice his chest. With one final swing, she slits his throat and leaves him for dead.

When Jordan finally stirs out of his sleep, he jumps out of bed and flicks the light switch. He grabs for his throat, glances down at his chest, and realizes he had been dreaming.

Jordan moves back to the bed and sits on the edge; he knows this dream means danger. The last time he had a bad dream like this was when his brother was shot.

Jordan glances at the clock. It was 9:30 p.m. and it has just dawned on him that he missed his dinner date with Jasmine.

Jasmine had paced the floor for hours. She could not understand why Jordan has stood her up. She was furious that he had not had the common curiosity to call and cancel. Anger continues to set in her mind as she makes her way to her bedroom where she begins stripping off her clothes. She pulls a nightshirt from her drawer and slips into it. She goes in to the bathroom and rinses her face of makeup. Jasmine was not accustomed to wearing makeup but by this being her first date with Jordan, she wanted to look her best, which ended up being a waste of time and makeup.

After Jasmine finishes up in the bathroom, she crawls beneath her comforter. She props her pillow up and relaxes her head trying to get comfortable but was unable to. Thoughts of Jordan fills her head; the happiness that she had felt earlier today about being with Jordan is now tempered with restraint, being made a fool of over a man once was enough to last her a lifetime.

~ clxii ~

Jordan sits on his chaise in his bedroom flicking through the TV channels. It was now 11:00 p.m. and he has yet to phone Jasmine to apologize for missing their dinner date. He knows he should have made the call sooner, but for some reason he was hesitant. It was something about Jasmine that puts fear in him. He knows that he has to tread water with her if not, he would fall fast for her.

Jasmine continues to lie in bed thinking of the curve that life had thrown her. One-step forward, three steps back. This seems to be the way her life has always gone, but she was determined not to let this little escapade get the best of her. If Jordan wants to play it like this, then she will show him that she is not the young naïve girl that she used to be and that she is not going to tolerate any bullshit from any man. True enough, he was the love of her life but just like she walked away from her marriage, she could easily walk away from him and not think twice about it.

Jordan rise early. He still feels bad about last night. He decides that he has to make it up to Jasmine. He showers, dresses and heads out. Minutes later, he pulls into the parking lot of O'Malley's and grabs a grocery cart on his way into the store. He could not decide on pancakes or waffles, so he gets both. He grabs a carton of eggs, maple syrup, sausage links and orange juice. On his way to the checkout counter, he walked pass the flower section and decides to grab a bouquet of flowers. He would have preferred roses but the selections were skimpy.

Jordan arrives at Jasmine just as the sun begins to creep through her blinds.

Jasmine rolls over reaches for the comforter that she has kicked off during the night and pulls it over her head. It is apparent that she had left her blinds opened last night. As she lay comfortably under the covers, she thinks she hears a knock at her front door. She removes the covers from her head and again she hears another knock. She glances at the clock on the nightstand. It is 8 a.m. in the morning. Who in the world would be knocking at her door this time of morning, she thinks.

Jasmine slips on her slippers, grabs her robe, and makes her way to the front door. When she opens the door, she gets the surprise of her life. Jordan stands with a bouquet of flowers in his hand looking sexier than ever.

"Jordan what are you doing here?"

"And good morning to you too, I'm here to apology for last night and to serve you breakfast in bed."

"Jordan, you do not have to do that."

"I know but I want to make it up to you and I want to let you know that I didn't stand you up on purpose."

"Well, if that's what you want to do, come on in."

~ clxiv ~

Jordan hands Jasmine the flowers and goes to his car to get the groceries.

Jasmine glances at herself in the mirror, "Oh my God, I look a hot mess."

When Jordan returns, he had two bags with him. Jasmine leads him to the kitchen and shows him where everything is. "Will you be okay while I shower?"

Jordan looks at her, "I said breakfast in bed so that means I'm serving you in bed."

"But Jordan, I look a hot mess."

"You look beautiful to me," Jordan says as he kisses her on the lips.

Jasmine throws her hands up," okay back to bed it is."

Jasmine lies in bed as the aroma of brewing coffee, eggs, sausage and pancakes filled her nostrils. She only hopes that the breakfast taste as good as it smells.

Twenty minutes later, Jordan enters her bedroom with a tray of food fit for a queen.

"Oh my Jordan, this looks and smells good."

"I wasn't sure if you wanted coffee or orange juice so I brought you both."

Jasmine sits up in bed as Jordan hands her the tray.

"Jordan thank you very much."

"Oh it's nothing it's the least I can do for standing you up. I hope you don't mind me sharing breakfast with you in bed?"

"No, I wouldn't mind that at all."

Jasmine didn't know how to feel right now. She was furious with Jordan last night and now, well she doesn't know what she is feeling, but she knows one thing, she is enjoying the unexpected company.

Jordan walks back into the room with his tray of food. He props the pillows up on the other side of the bed and makes himself comfortable.

"I must say this is delicious." "A man who knows his way around the kitchen gets an A in my book."

"I'm glad to hear that. So does this mean you forgive me for yesterday?"

"I don't know, ask me later."

"Jasmine, I am truly sorry, but to be honest I fell asleep and when I woke it was 9:00 p.m. I know I should have called you then but I was afraid you would not talk to me."

"I see, but you should have called anyway. To me that is the most respectful thing to do in a situation like that. I would have been disappointed but I would have appreciated the call, but you left me to assume the worst."

~ clxvi ~

"And that is?"

"That you did not want to be bothered."

"One thing that you will learn about me is that if I do not want to be bothered, I will tell you. I believe in being honest when dealing with someone feelings."

"Trust me, people do this kind of thing all the time because they do not want to be bothered but they do not have the guts to tell a person. I was married to a man for years and to this day, I do not know why he married me. He already had a family here before we married and I knew nothing about them. The first three months of my marriage was perfect and then after that, everything started to go downhill. I started to see a person that I did not like but being the fool that I was I stayed even when he beat me to the point I had to be hospitalized and lost the child that I carried for three months. He was disrespectful in public and behind closed doors. The breaking point was when I found out about his sons and their mother and that he had moved them from Indianapolis to Florida. After five months into our marriage he had bought them a house two streets over from where we lived."

"That's deep." "How did you find out about them?"

"His baby's mother came to our home one morning. I guess she was sitting outside waiting for him to leave for work. I was on my way out the door when I spotted her walking up our walkway. She introduced herself to me and began to fill me in on what was going on. I guess she got tired of being the other woman. I was shocked at first but the more I thought about it the more things became clearer.

A couple of my neighbors had told me a few years ago that they had seen Ricky working in a woman's yard a couple of streets over and again I did not pay any attention. During our marriage, Ricky spent a lot of time with his friend that I never met who lived two streets over. He spent more time there then he did at home. I was always alone at night. But knowing what I know now, he was spending the time he should have been spending with his wife. He was spending it with his sons and their mother. Don't t get me wrong, I would not have any problems with him spending time with his boys, but that was just wrong for him to keep them a secret from me. He was doing more than spending time with his boys, but now I am not that naïve and foolish women anymore. I will not tolerate bullshit from any man and if a man doesn't treat me the way I want to be treated, he can consider himself history."

"Well, I'm sorry that you had to go through that. If I had known you were going through that shit, I would have come to Florida myself and brought you home. I will always treat you the way a beautiful woman like yourself should be treated."

Denise Hill

CHAPTER 19

After breakfast, Jordan removes the trays and is in the kitchen doing the dishes while Jasmine showers. They decide to spend the day together.

Jasmine dresses and they head out. On the way to the car, Jasmine asks Jordan if he has started his Christmas shopping.

"Nope, I haven't even thought about it, but since you mentioned it, why don't we head over to the fashion mall. I 'm pretty sure I can pick up a few things there.

"Sounds good to me, I just love to shop."

"I just bet you do. What woman doesn't?" Jordan replies.

Danielle drops the boys off at her moms. Donnie and she agree to meet at his hotel and talk.

Brenda pulls into the parking lot of the hotel. She gets out and makes her way inside. She waits for the elevator as she thinks of a way to keep Donnie and Danielle apart. She has to think quick. She knows Danielle could pull up at any minute. When she spoke with Donnie this morning, he told her that they were meeting at his hotel to talk things over.

~ clxx ~

The elevator door opens and Brenda hops in. She pushes the button to take her to Donnie's floor. Brenda rides up to the eighth floor. She is a little hesitant to get out but she knows this is her only chance.

Brenda makes her way down the hall to Donnie's room. She knocks twice before Donnie opens the door.

Brenda what are you doing here?" Donnie nervously asks. I told you that Danielle was stopping by."

"I know, I 'm sorry, I won't stay long, I just have to use your restroom."

"Alright but make it quick."

Donnie begins to pace back and forth. He did not want Danielle showing up while Brenda was here because it would only make matters worse.

Danielle pulls into the parking lot of the Hampton Inn. She rides the elevator up to the eighth floor. She is a little nervous about this visit. She hopes by this evening, Donnie will be back home where he belongs.

Danielle walks down the hall until she comes to Donnie's room. She knocks twice and then a third time and is on her fourth knock when Donnie opens the door.

"Hey Danielle come on in." Donnie is so glad to see Danielle with a smile on her face that he has forgotten all about Brenda.

As Danielle moves further into the room, the bathroom door opens and there stands Brenda naked.

"What the fuck is going on Donnie? I came all the way over here thinking we were going to talk and work things out between us and you have this bitch up in here."

Donnie stands there with his mouth wide open. He is in shock.

"Donnie I'm through, if you want this stank bitch, then you can have her."

"Who are you calling a stank bitch. Don't hate me because I've fucked your husband good," Brenda says as she proceeds to put her clothes back on.

"Listen here you simple minded fuck. Just because you sucked his dick a couple of times, you will have to come with more than that to truly satisfy a real man. Everything is not always about sex, as you seem to think. You dumb bitch."

Before Brenda could say another word, Danielle bashes her in the mouth. Danielle throws another punch that hits her smack dead in the eye.

Donnie runs over to where they both stand and gets in the middle. Danielle continues to throw punches to Brenda's face left and right. There was so much commotion going on that security is called up to Donnie's room where eventually the police show up. When the police arrive, one officer talks with Brenda and the other one speaks with Danielle and Donnie.

Donnie explains to the officer what has happened, that Brenda had no reason to be there, and that she was only there to cause trouble.

The officer that is with Brenda walks over to Danielle and Donnie to inform them that Brenda is pressing charges against Danielle and therefore he would have to arrest Danielle on assault and battery charges.

"What, you have got to be fucking kidding me?" Danielle yells.

"Mrs., watch your mouth and calm down. I am going to have to ask you to turn around and put your hands behind your back."

"All come on sir, you don't have to do this. I told you Brenda brought this on herself", Donnie says as he pleads with the officer.

"Sir, I am just doing my job."

"Donnie get Matthew on the phone," Danielle says.

The officer places Danielle in the back of the police car as he waits for his partner to finish up with Brenda.

Matthew steps out of the shower just as his phone rings.

"Hey Matthew, this is Donnie, Danielle is being arrested on assault and battery charges. She and Brenda got into a fight and Brenda has decided to press charges against her."

"What, what the fuck have you gotten my sister into?"

"I'll explain everything, but right now we need you to meet us downtown.

Matthew hangs up from Donnie and explains what Donnie had told him to his wife Monica as he gets dress.

"Monica whatever you do, do not call Mom. I need you to get Jordan on the phone and tell him to meet me downtown."

Jordan had just finished picking up a couple of gifts for his mom when his phone rings.

"What?" Alright, I'm on my way."

"Is everything okay?"

"No, we have to go; I will drop you off on the way. Danielle just got arrested for assault and battery charges so I need to head downtown."

"Oh my God," Jasmine says. "I want to go with you Jordan."

"Are you sure?"

"Yes."

Brenda is on her way to the emergency room to have her face looked at. The paramedics think it would be in her best interest to have a doctor look at her mouth and nose along with her black eye.

Donnie met Matthew at the station. Matthew was able to go back and check on Danielle to make sure she is all right. Being that Matthew had been a detective for twelve years, he has a lot of pull in the department. He was able to get Danielle OR out without the long process.

When he arrives back to the lobby, Jordan and Jasmine have arrived.

Within twenty minutes, Danielle is released and is on her way to the lobby.

Feeling ashamed and embarrassed, Danielle breaks down when she sees the look on her brother's face.

Jordan and Matthew met her halfway and embraced her. "Don't cry. It's okay now, I'll take you home," Jordan says.

CHAPTER 20

Brenda catches a cab from the emergency room to the Hampton Inn to pick up her car.

After being examined by the doctor, Brenda is told that not only did she have a black eye, a busted lip, but she also has suffered a broken nose.

Too ashamed to return to her mother's, Brenda checks into a motel down the street from the Hampton Inn.

In the meantime, Danielle decides to ride back home with Jordan and Jasmine.

They ride home in silence. Danielle lays her head back against the seat and tries to relax her mind but there are so many thoughts running through her head about the incident that had taken place earlier. She tries to figure out in her mind how she could ever forgive Donnie for the trouble he had caused.

The more she thought about the situation, the more she realizes that if she had not brought Brenda into their lives this would have never happened. She is as much to blame as Donnie.

Jordan pulls into their driveway while Matthew and Donnie follow behind him.

Once inside the house, everyone takes a seat on the couch in the family room. There were no words exchanged but it was obvious that there was some explaining that needed to be done.

Donnie takes the floor and explains everything from beginning to the end.

"So you're telling me that you thought Brenda was me that night?"

"Yes, that is what I'm saying you can either believe me or not I have no reason to lie to you. I have never been attracted to her anyway whatsoever. When you first brought the idea to me about Brenda living with us, you know I was against him it from the get-go. I thought she was sneaky and conniving then. Danielle you know I would never do anything to hurt you. You should know me better than that. You know we have had our difficulties but there has never been any reason for me to venture out when you can give me all that I need. It's on you now Danielle to believe me or not, I've said all I have to say."

"I don't know right now, I need some time to think about everything that has happened."

"I think you guys need sometime alone to work this out. Danielle I know you are hurt but Donnie is your husband and the father of your kids. You can't let some woman that you have known for less than a year come into your lives and destroy that," Jordan says as he takes a hold of sister's hands.

~ clxxviii ~

"Well she also should think about contacting an attorney. If Brenda doesn't follow through with the assault and battery charges, I'm afraid the state my pick up your case. But knowing Brenda, she will see this through," Matthew says.

Donnie arrives back at his hotel. As he gets out of his car, Brenda approaches him. "Look at what your wife has done to me. That bitch will pay for this," Brenda yells.

"You brought all of this shit on yourself; you had no reason to be here when you knew she was stopping by. Just like now, you have no reason to be here. You need to leave Brenda."

"Donnie I know you don't mean that, you need me whether you believe it or not. Danielle doesn't love you like I do."

"If you do not leave Brenda, I will call the police and get a restraining order against you. Now you can believe that or not."

"Well you tell Danielle payback is a bitch and that she better not make any problems for me at work."

Donnie continues to walk inside the hotel ignoring Brenda. He knows she is conniving but now she is taking this a little too far threatening his wife.

Inside Donnie's hotel room, he picks up the phone to call Danielle. He wants her to know that Brenda is making threats against her.

"Danielle I think we both need to go and file restraining order against her just in case she tries anything."

"I agree I know some of the girls in the office had once told me that Brenda has some physiological issues. At the time I thought they were just being mean."

Later that evening, Danielle stops by her mom to pick up the boys. When she arrives, she notices that the gang is all there. Her heart began to beat rapidly afraid of what she would learn once she enters the house. It was unusual for all of her siblings to be at her mom's at the same time unless there was something going on. Her first thought was something had happened to her mother and then her kids.

Danielle rush inside to find her family gathered around the fireplace having a good time. What a relief she thinks to herself.

"Are you guys having a party without me?"

Mark walks over to her and hugs her. He whispers in her ear, "Way to go baby girl, but next time try not to get arrested."

"Come here you poor girl. Are you okay?" Mrs. Daniels asks.

"I'm fine mom." "Donnie called and told me that Brenda showed up at his hotel again and started making threats against me. He suggested that we go and get a restraining order against her."

~ clxxx ~

"That girl is crazy," Theresa says.

"Donnie is right. You guys need to do that as soon as possible. If you would like, I can meet you guys downtown first thing Monday morning," Matthew says.

"Let me check with Donnie to see if that is okay with him."

"Don't wait too long Danielle," Mrs. Daniels told her.

"Do you have a gun Danielle?" Jordan asks.

"No, and I don't need one."

"Yes you do, take a look at Brenda's rap sheet. This woman is crazy!"

Danielle looks at the rap sheet and is shocked to learn that Brenda had done this kind of thing several times before. She also learns that Brenda has spent two years in a mental institution.

"Oh my God, how in the world did my employer not know this before they hired her?"

"This is why it is very important that you and Donnie get that restraining order because something tells me that you have not seen the last of her," Matthew says.

"I'm sorry to break up this party, but I have to leave. I have an important lady waiting for me," Jordan says.

"And who might that be?" Theresa asks.

Jordan laughs, "It's for me to know and for you not to find out."

"Go ahead with your bad self," Mark comments.

Jordan gives his mom a kiss on the cheek before leaving. "Danielle, I will check on you tomorrow."

Later that night, Danielle phones Donnie and fills him in on what she has found about Brenda.

"Danielle, I 'm coming home right now, I want to be there for you and the boys. I don't trust Brenda to leave you guys there alone."

Jordan arrives at six thirty as planned. He has arranged for them to have dinner at St. Elmo's. He had to pull some strings to get them in at such a short notice but he is friends with the manager on duty.

Jasmine wonders if Jordan will actually show up this time but when he does, she is grateful. She would not have made any more plans with him.

Jasmine watch as Jordan makes his way to her front door; masculinity stands out even from the distance.

Jasmine allows Jordan to knock three times before she opens the door. She did not want him to know that she has been standing at the door peering out the window waiting on his arrival.

When Jordan lays eyes on Jasmine, his heart is doing its own dance. "Damn she looks good!" he says.

Jasmine is dressed in her brown fitted suede dress and her brown suede boots that she had planned to wear yesterday for their date. The fitted dress shows every curve possible and Jordan is loving every bit of it.

Jordan leads Jasmine down the walkway to his car. She did not want to be affected by his magnetism because she did not trust him completely. Her experience with men makes her very leery, but this was Jordan, a man she has known practically all her life.

When they arrive at the restaurant, the host comes out to greet them and removes two menus from the slot. "Two?" the host asks.

"Yes," Jordan answers.

The young woman in her early twenties smiles at her with appreciation.

"Follow me."

Jordan is well known in the community. As they walk heads turns. Whispers follow.

The waiter arrives within minutes. "Would you care for a drink before we order dinner?" Jordan asks.

"Yes," Jasmine says as she gives her drink order to the waiter.

Jordan and Jasmine look over the menu.

"What are you going to have?" Jasmine asks.

"My usual, a rack of lamb, steamed green beans with mashed potatoes and gravy."

"Um, that sounds good; I think I'll have the same."

Dinner went well. The two talked about their different experiences in life when Jasmine gets up enough nerves to ask Jordan why he had broken off his engagement with Vanessa.

"Thomas and I had been at a bar drinking and watching the game. We both decided that we had had too much to drink to drive home. The owner suggested that I leave my car and catch a cab, but I decide to give Vanessa a call and just have her pick us up and drop us off at my home. So, that is what I did. We both were drunk, which normally does not happen with me.

Back at the house, Vanessa makes sure that we both get in the house safe, I kiss her good bye and she leaves, so I thought. Thomas crashes in one of my guest rooms while I take a shower to try to sober up. When I got out of the shower, I laid across the bed when I hear noise coming from the bedroom next to mine. At first, it sounds like a television but I know there is no television in that room. I hear the noise again, so I walk outside my room and I could have sworn I hear Vanessa voice coming from the room that Thomas is in. By this time, I am thinking that I am really losing it. I was headed back inside my room when I hear her voice again. I knew I was not just hearing things, so I approach the door turn the knob and hit the light switch and there I find Vanessa in bed with Thomas."

"What did they do?"

"There was nothing for them to do but leave before I did something that would have landed me in jail or should I say prison."

The next morning I had Danielle take me back to the bar to retrieve my car and when I returned. I had several calls from them both apologizing and saying that this was something that just happened, but now that I look back on things, I wondered how long this had been going on behind my back. I remember on several occasion when I would throw parties at my home, I would sometimes find Vanessa and Thomas off in the corner to themselves."

"When did this happen?"

"It was about two months ago."

"And you stayed with her after this had happened?"

"Yes, I did, but don't ask me why because I really couldn't tell you. When I realized that I would never find happiness as long as I was with her, I broke off the engagement."

"Did you continue your friendship with Thomas?"

"No, not really. He is my accounting manager and that's it. He is the person you will be working with."

"You mean he works for you?"

"Yes, if I had it my way I would have fired him after I caught him with Vanessa."

"Is it hard for you to see him on a daily basis?"

"Sometimes, but I try to avoid him as much as possible."

"That's too bad being that this is your company and you have to try to avoid someone you don't want to see. I think I would have taken my chances and fired his ass and if he wanted to sue me than let him."

Jordan laughs, "You amaze me. I would have never thought you would have had that kind of attitude."

"Honey life has a way of changing your attitude and the way you think about people and things."

"Now that we have gotten that out of the way, what would you like to do now?"

"Why don't we go back to my place for some drinks and a little jazz?"

~ clxxxvi ~

Jordan lifted a brow as he glances at her. "Are you serious?" Alcohol and a beautiful woman don't mix."

Jasmine burst out laughing," Jordan you are so crazy."

"Why don't we go to my place to listen to some Jazz and have a couple of drinks by the fireplace?"

"That sounds even better," Jasmine say."

CHAPTER 21

Donnie checks out of his hotel room at eight thirty. When he arrives home, he notices that all four of Danielle's tires have been slashed.

He runs into the house he finds his boys asleep and kisses them both on the forehead before searching for Danielle. Donnie checks their bedroom and sees the light coming from the bathroom.

Donnie enters the bathroom and calls out to Danielle. Danielle pulls back the shower curtain to see Donnie standing there with a frighten look on his face.

"What's wrong?" Danielle asks.

"Someone has slashed all four of your tires on your truck."

"You have got to be kidding me."

"No, I'm serious we need to call the police and file a police report so this will be on file."

"Can you hand me that towel."

Donnie tries with all his power not to stare at the two firm breast right before his eyes as he hands his wife the towel.

Danielle notices how her husband is looking at her as she wraps the towel around her naked body while trying to hide the smile that threatens to show.

"Why don't you go and call the police while I get dressed." Danielle says.

Donnie phones the police and decides to let Matthew know what was going on.

Minutes later, Matthew arrives just as the police pull up.

Matthew identifies himself as a detective and explains everything that has happened earlier. The officers checked the house inside and out just to make sure there were no broken windows or no forced entries.

They suggested that Donnie and Danielle go down and get a restraining order against Brenda.

After the officers had gone, Danielle goes into the house to check on her boys. Donnie and Matthew continue to stand outside on the porch.

"I think it would be wise if you changed the locks on the house as soon as possible and until that has been done, I would sleep with one eye opened," Matthew says.

"Man don't say that." "I'm just being realistic. Brenda's rap sheet is no joke, so you guys need to take every precaution when dealing with her.

~ CXC ~

I told Danielle that I would meet you guys downtown on Monday morning to get that restraining order."

"Not only do we need to get that restraining order, but we need to contact an attorney for Danielle and go to the boys' school and get Brenda's name off our pick up list."

"Yeah, that is a must."

"Well, I am going to head home. If anything else should happen, which I hope it doesn't for Brenda's sake; do not hesitate to call me. Tell Danielle that I will talk with her tomorrow."

"Alright, thanks for stopping by."

"Are the boys still asleep?" Donnie asks Danielle.

"Yes. They are sound asleep."

"Matthew told me to tell you that he will call you tomorrow. I told him that we should go to the boys' school Monday and remove Brenda's name off of our pick-up list."

"I forgot about that. I am so glad you remembered."

When Jordan and Jasmine arrive back at his place, Jordan tells her to make herself comfortable. Jordan lit the fireplace and put on his favorite Paul Taylor CD. Jordan walks back to the kitchen and grabs a couple of coolers. Jordan fixes himself a drink and takes a seat next to Jasmine. He hands her a peach cooler while he sips on some Patron.

Jasmine feels so comfortable with Jordan; she could easily see herself as Mrs. Daniels. "Jordan tell me something. Are you truly over Vanessa or are you angry that she cheated?"

"I still love Vanessa in my own way, but I'm not in love with her. I don't even have any respect for her anymore."

"Do you still love your ex?"

"No, the love that I had for him was gone years ago. I think the reason I stayed as long as I did was I did not want to say that I failed at being a good wife. But no matter how good of a wife I could have been, it would not have mattered. My marriage ended when I lost my child. I began to hang out with my friends because Ricky was always gone. We very seldom went anywhere together. Now when I look back, I feel so stupid, but I guess you live and learn."

Jordan did not say anything. He just shook his head in agreement with her.

Jordan moves closer to Jasmine on the couch. He grabs a hold of her hand as he looks at her. There was something intoxicating about her presence. Looking at her lush figure and images of her naked in his arms flashed through his mind. He tries so hard to control the urge to kiss her but he lost that battle.

Leaning over he pressed a kiss to her cheek. Lowering his head, he took her mouth; gently his tongue parted her lips. Jordan caused her body and mind to react in all sorts of ways. Everything about him has turned her on.

Jordan lingers in the kiss energy pulsing from his heart into his limbs willing life into his manhood. He could not help but imagine himself between her thighs. He wants to give into the waves of emotions flooding between them but knows this was not the right time so he pulls himself away from her.

Feeling rejected, Jasmine glances at her watch. It's getting late, I think we should call it a night."

Jordan walks Jasmine to her front door. He kisses her on the lips and says good night.

Inside, Jasmine watch through her front window as Jordan drives off. It was something about the way he said that he still loved Vanessa that bothers her. She begins to have mix feelings about getting involved.

Jordan pulls his Mercedes into his driveway. He climbs out a few minutes later, braving the cold November night. He could not help but wonder if Jasmine was disappointed that he ended their kiss, but little did she know, that if he had not ended it they would have ended up in his bed.

It was late when Donnie and Danielle crawl into bed. Danielle did not realize how much she missed sharing a bed with her husband. Just lying next to him, she feels the tension seeping out of her muscles and the stress she had not recognized ease from her mind. She continues to lie in her husband's arms until they both were fast asleep.

The next morning, Donnie had replaced all of Danielle's slashed tires with brand new ones.

When Danielle awoke, the locksmith was there replacing their locks.

Donnie was in the kitchen preparing breakfast for his family. Donnie was glad to back home but things were far from being back to normal. He realizes that if he was in Danielle's shoes, he is not sure he would be able to handle what has happened. He knows they will have to take things one day at a time, but his first priority was keeping his family safe.

Donnie had the table set for breakfast. He asks Danielle to go and get the boys. When the boys find out that their dad has prepared breakfast for them, they take off running and collide with the locksmith.

"Daddy, Daddy," the boys yell in unison. It touched Donnie's heart to see his boys running to him with tears in their eyes. Donnie kneels down, grabs both boys in his arms, and hugs them tightly. "Okay, it's time to eat," Danielle says smiling.

Jasmine arrives just as church was about to begin. She spots her parents up front. She makes her way to the second pew and ease in next to her mom. Her parents are surprised and thrilled that she has decided to join them.

~ cxciv ~

Jordan arrives late. He scans the room and finds the only available pew in the back of the church and takes his seat. It has been a while since he attended Mount Olive Missionary Baptist church but he feels the need to be here today.

Vanessa sees Jordan when he walks in and waited for the right time to get up and take a seat next to him. Jordan acknowledges her and continues listening to the sermon.

After the service, Jasmine says her good byes to her parents and is on her way out when she notices Jordan and Vanessa sitting together. She gives Jordan a weak smile and continues walking. By the time she makes it to her car, she is in tears. Jordan runs out after her and calls her name but Jasmine continues to unlock her door she gets in and drives away.

Jasmine enters her apartment and heads for the bathroom. She ignores the phone ringing in the background. The last thing that she wants is to talk with Jordan. She has no time for any of his excuses. Jasmine opens the medicine cabinet and grabs the bottle of Tylenol. She makes her way to the kitchen where she pours herself a glass of water and pops two pills. She needs relief from the throbbing headache.

Jasmine walks back down the hall to her bedroom where she dresses down to her slip and lays across her bed.

The dark clouds looming over Indianapolis, the twenty-five degree temperature matched Jordan's mood as he pulls out of the church's parking lot. He knows how things must have looked to Jasmine, but it was innocent. He tries phoning her on her cell but no answer. He figures he will give her time to get home and then he will try calling her at home.

Jordan has phoned Jasmine several times. He decides after three calls and no answer that he would leave her a voice message before heading over to his mom's for her weekly Sunday dinner.

Jordan pulls up in front of his mothers. It was obvious that he was the last to arrive judging by the lack of parking space. Jordan walks in to find that his family has started without him.

"Thanks for waiting for me guys."

"Sorry sweetheart, I didn't know if you were coming or not," Mrs. Daniels says.

"Mom, how many of your Sunday dinners have I missed?"

"Well Jasmine wasn't here but now that's she back I didn't know if you had made dinner plans with her."

"Hey bro, what's up with you? You don't seem like yourself." Mark asks.

"Oh, I am having a little trouble with a woman right now."

"Are you and Jasmine at each other already?" Mark asks.

"It seems to be that way. Jasmine saw Vanessa and I sitting together at church, but I did not come with Vanessa. Vanessa came and sat down beside me half way through the service.

"Did you tell Jasmine that?" Danielle asks.

"I didn't get a chance to tell her anything. I called her several times but she never picked up."

After Dinner, Donnie takes the boys home with him so that Danielle can stop by and visit Jasmine.

"Hey Danielle let Jasmine know that I will be in the office at nine if she still wants to stop by."

CHAPTER 22

Jasmine lies across her bed sleep when Danielle knocks at her door. Danielle had knocked several times before calling Jasmine on the phone. Danielle was about to leave when Jasmine opens the door.

"Well, it's about time; I've been out here banging on your door for about fifteen minutes. I thought your neighbors were about to call the cops on me," Danielle says as she enters the apartment.

"Why didn't you call me?"

"I did, but you didn't answer."

"I'm sorry, I must have been knocked out."

Danielle removes her coat and gloves, "Girl it is cold as hell out there, I should have gone straight home after dinner. Oh, before I forget, Jordan told me to tell you that he will be in the office tomorrow at nine if you still want to stop by."

Jasmine did not respond.

"I see you are in the same mood Jordan's in."

"I do not want to talk about Jordan right now, if you don't mind."

"Jordan told us what happened at church. He said he did not come with Vanessa. She came and sat down with him halfway through the service, if that makes you feel any better."

"You know what?" "I can't seem to win for losing. It is obvious that Jordan cannot tell Vanessa to stay the hell away from him. He even had the nerve to tell me last night that he still loved her in his own way. Now what kind of shit is that even if that is how he feels? He should not tell someone that when you are out on a date with them."

Danielle could not say anything because she agrees with Jasmine.

"All I can say is just take it slow with him and don't put your heart into it right away. I know that Jordan cares deeply for you. Hell, everyone that knows him knows that. So I do not know what his trip is. Unless he is afraid to get close to you fearing that he may get his heart broken again."

"But Jordan needs to realize that he is not the first and will not be the last person that has gotten their heart broken. I have had my heart broken twice, once by him and then my ex. I refuse to let it happen again and if that means I will be alone for the rest of my life, then so be it."

"That's my girl. You know I like the new Jasmine better than the old one."

~ CC ~

"Why is that?"

"Because the new Jasmine is not naïve and will stand up for herself." "That's why." "There are too many women out here that will believe anything a man tells them, and put up with anything just to have a man. How pitiful. I like it that you do not rely on a man to take care of you either."

"If I waited for a man to take care of me, I would be out on the street".

"Now that you have been all up in my business, what is going on with you and Donnie?"

"Girl, I didn't call and tell you that Donnie is back home and when he arrived home he found all four of my tires slashed. That Brenda is a crazy bitch. Matthew pulled a rap sheet on her and found out that she has had restraining orders against her twice and that she has spent two years in a mental institution."

"You are kidding me."

"I'm meeting with my boss tomorrow afternoon and to let her know that I have a restraining order against Brenda and to let her know about her rap sheet. If Karen knew about this, I know she would have never hired her. Donnie moved back in when I told him about her rap sheet and since she has made threats to Donnie about getting back at me. Girl, you should have seen the boys this morning when I told them that their dad had made breakfast for them. It was so touching. To be honest I am glad to have my husband back. I slept like a baby in his arms last night."

"Well good for you guys and the next time. Do not allow a bitch up in your house even I know better than that."

They both laugh.

"Girl I know that's right Ms. Jazzy Jas."

"Oh my God. I haven't heard any one call me that in years."

"I had forgotten all about it until just now," Danielle said.

"Now back to Jordan. What are you going to do about him?"

"I don't know."

"Are you going to show up tomorrow for your interview with him?"

"I haven't decided."

"Jasmine don't let anything stand in your way that will benefit you, not even Jordan."

"You're right; I know how to work with someone but stay out of their way at the same time."

Jasmine and Danielle talked for another hour before Danielle decides to head home.

"Call me tomorrow and let me know how things turn out," Danielle says as she walks to the door.

"You know I will."

"Tell Donnie and the boys I said hi."

Danielle kisses Jasmine on the cheek, "Danielle please be careful."

Jasmine stands in the door and watches as Danielle drives off.

The next morning, Jasmine is dressed and ready to go. She has second thoughts about going, but decides to go anyway. She puts away her pride for now because she knows she has to do what is best for her.

When Jasmine arrives, she takes the elevator to the sixteenth floor. Her heart is beating a mile a minute. She has instilled in her mind that this would be about the job and nothing else. She told herself over again that she did not care about Jordan and Vanessa; somehow, she wished her heart would believe that.

When the elevators doors open, she was hesitant to step out. If it was not for the others in the elevator, she would have ridden the elevator back down.

Jasmine makes her way to the receptionist, "Hello, I have an appointment with Mr. Daniels."

"What is your name and what time is your appointment?" asks the receptionist.

"I'm Jasmine Smith and my appointment is for nine o'clock."

"Please have a seat and I'll let Mr. Daniels know you're here."

Jasmine takes a seat on the leather couch as the receptionist notifies Jordan that she is here.

Jordan appears out of nowhere. He stands at the receptionist desk looking like he had just stepped off the cover of GQ magazine. He is dressed in a gray pinstriped Armani suit with matching shoes.

"Why in the world does he have to look so damn good this morning?" Jasmine asks herself.

"Good morning, Jasmine," Jordan says with his deep sexy voice.

Immediately, she tries to ignore the heat that touched her body when the corners of his lips curved.

"Good morning Jordan," Jasmine says as she stands.

Jordan motions for her to follow him. As the two walk down the hall to his office, Jasmines can smell Jordan's cologne which starts to turn her on. The one thing that turns her on is a good smelling man. She eyes Jordan out of the corner of her eye and catches him starring at her. Jordan chuckles while Jasmines rolls her eyes. He is so arrogant she thinks.

Inside his office, he gestures for her to take a seat in the empty chair as he moves to take his seat behind his desk.

"First things first. I want to explain to you about yesterday at church. It was not what it seemed. I did not come with Vanessa nor did I sit with her. She spotted me halfway through the service and decided to sit next to me."

"Jordan you do not have to explain anything to me. What you do is your business. You are a single man, remember."

Jordan could tell by the tone of Jasmine's voice that she is a little salty with him.

"Is that so, Jasmine? You mean to tell me that it wouldn't bother you if I dated you and other women?"

The look on her face told it all.

Before Jasmine could say a word, Jordan burst out laughing. I am sorry, I 'm just messing with you Jasmine. I do not date more than one woman at a time." Jasmine is furious she doesn't think this was funny at all. She sat there with a straight face not blinking an eye.

"Are you through with your jokes?"

Jordan is tickled. He thinks Jasmine looks sexier when she is angry.

"Yes, I am through with my jokes. Now let us get down to business. Jordan explains the job in great details to Jasmine. She knows this will be a challenge for her but she gladly accepts the position.

"I have asked Thomas to come in early today to get you set up for training. My secretary will work on getting your office organized and in the meantime, I have some paperwork for you to fill out." Jordan hands Jasmine a folder. After you completed your paperwork, I will show you around."

"Okay, sounds good to me."

"If you will excuse me for a minute, I want to check to make sure Thomas is here."

Jasmine begins to fill out the paperwork. She was not so sure if she can work so close to Jordan without having feelings for him. If he looks the way he looks today, she is going to have problems.

Denise Hill

CHAPTER 23

Donnie and Danielle dropped the boys off at school. They have spoken to the principal and removed Brenda's name off their pick- up list. They are now heading downtown to meet Matthew to file for a restraining order.

Brenda sits parked down the street. She waits for Donnie and Danielle to leave before approaching the house. She pulls out her key but is unable to get the door open. She makes her way around back to the back door; still she is unable to open the door. "Damn, they must have changed the locks," she says aloud

Brenda looks around the backyard for something that can possibly break the back window. She searches until she comes up on one of the boy's remote control truck.

"This will have to do." She smashes the truck against the window. It breaks and she removes the pieces of glass that remain in the window so that she will not cut herself. She reaches inside to get a hold of the knob and unlocks the door.

As she makes her way inside, she thinks she hears a car pull up and immediately runs back to the boys' bedroom and hid inside the closet. She waits for few minutes before coming out.

Brenda goes to the family room and glance out the window but there is no one in sight. She goes to the kitchen, grabs a knife, and heads back to the family room where she begins to slice their leather couch. When she is satisfied, she goes to Donnie's favorite chair and begins to slice it also. She pulls a tube of lipstick from her purse, moves to the wall, and begins writing the word bitch in red lipstick.

Once she completes her task, she makes her way back to the back door and is gone.

After filing for a restraining order, Matthew hands Danielle a business card. "Attorney James Taylor is recommended by my boss. I have already talked with him about your situation. He is expecting you today at eleven."

"Thanks Matthew, I will be there, but first I have to stop by my job and talk with my boss and let her know what's going on."

"Okay, but let me know how the meeting goes with James."

"I will and thanks again for everything."

Donnie and Danielle are on their way to talk with her boss when Danielle receives a call from one of her neighbors. "Hey Danielle, I just wanted to let that you know that I just saw Brenda leave your house. I saw her coming from the backyard so I thought I would let you know."

"Thanks, Darlene."

"Darlene says she has seen Brenda at the house. She says she saw her coming from the backyard. Why don't we make a detour and go check out the house."

"She can't get in Danielle."

"I know, but I will feel better if we stopped by just to make sure."

Donnie and Danielle arrived home. When they enter the house, Danielle's hand goes to her chest, "Oh my God, I can't believe this bitch."

Donnie pulls out his cell and phones the police. "I swear if the police don't do something, I will get this bitch myself."

"I need to call the attorney and let him know what has happened and that I will be late."

After speaking with Mr. Taylor, Danielle calls Matthew.

"Your neighbor saw her coming from the backyard?"

"Yes." "I thought you guys had the locks changed."

"We did."

"Have you checked the back door? Never mind I'm on my way." Make sure that you do not touch anything. Hopefully we will be able to get some finger prints."

Matthew arrives the same time as the police. "Hey Daniels, what are you doing here?" one of the officers asked.

~ CCX ~

"This is my sister's house. She has had some issues with a woman who was seen leaving her house this morning."

Matthew walks around to the back of the house where he sees the back door window has been broken. He makes his way back to his car and grabs his tool kit. When he returns he put on gloves and begins to dust for fingerprints. When he finishes, he enters the house from the back. "Hey, how did you get in?" Danielle asks.

"Brenda broke the back door window."

Matthew walks over to the kitchen counter and holds up a knife, "Did anyone of you have this knife?" Donnie and Danielle look at each other and shake their heads no. Matthew wraps the knife up and places it inside a plastic bag. "I'm going to take this in and have it checked for fingerprints. I dusted the backdoor knob and pieces of the glass that was scattered around for fingerprints. If they come back as a match for Brenda, I will get an arrest warrant for her. What is Brenda's mother's address?"

After Jasmine completes her paperwork, Jordan shows her around the office. Once the tour was completed, they stop in front of an empty office. Jordan hands her a set of keys, "This is your new office you can do with it as you see fit."

Jasmine moves inside the office. She turns back to look at Jordan, "I can't believe how spacious this office is. Jordan thanks for everything."

"You're more than welcome. Now if you do not mind, I will need to pass you off to Thomas so that he can get you set up for your training tomorrow. I will be out of this office the rest of the week, but if you need anything, do not hesitate to call me, or you can let Ronnie know. Ronnie's office is the one right next to mine. He is out today but will be back in the office tomorrow."

"Are you on your way out right now?"

"Yes, is there something you need?"

"No, I was just curious."

"I will check with you from time to time to see how things are going."

"Okay, I guess I'll see you later."

"Oh, by the way, Thomas will introduce you to everyone tomorrow."

Jordan walks Jasmine over to Thomas's office. Jordan and Thomas are cordial to each other but Jasmine can sense the tension between the two.

By noon, Thomas has Jasmine set up for her training for the rest of the week.

"I guess this just about does it," Thomas says. You are free to go if you do not have any questions."

"No, I do not have any questions."

"I will see you tomorrow morning."

"Okay, thanks Thomas. But before I leave I want to go and check out my new office again."

Thomas smiles as Jasmine walks away.

On her way to her car, Jasmine pulls out her cell phone and dials Danielle.

"Hey girl, I went for my interview with Jordan. You will not believe how big my office is."

"You have your own office?"

"Yes, can you believe that"?

"Yes, Jasmine you are dealing with Jordan. You know he will take care of you. Hey can I call you later, I'm getting ready to walk into the attorney's office."

"Don't forget," Jasmine says.

"You know I won't. I have got something to tell you."

Jasmine was on her way to have lunch with her mom when her cell rings.

"How did things go?" Jordan asks.

"Everything went fine; I'm so excited I can't wait until I can decorate my office."

Jordan laughs. He is happy to know that Jasmine is excited about working for him.

"Again, I want to thank you for everything, Jordan."

"Well, I will talk with you later. I just wanted to make sure everything was okay with you."

"Alright Jordan, talk with you later."

Jasmine was a little disappointed that Jordan has not said anything about them getting together.

Jasmine will have to get her feeling under control while working with him.

On the ride home, Jordan tries to remember the last time he has been intimate with a woman. It had only been a week since he broke off the engagement with Vanessa, but they had stopped being intimate with each other way before her betrayal. After Jordan finds out that she had been secretly taking birth control pills he had no desire to be intimate with her or any woman but seeing Jasmine this morning brought those feelings to the forefront. He is hit with a rush of pleasure. He has been overcome with a weird feeling and although he has been able to downplay it and get through the interview session without her knowing it had been there.

He wants to tell Jasmine just how he feels about her how he wants to brush his lips against hers to taste her and bury himself deep inside her. He has it bad for her and wonders how he is going to control himself while working with her.

Alexis pulls into Jordan's driveway she lets herself in with the key that he had given her. When she enters the home, she hears the television coming from the kitchen. She makes her way to the kitchen where she finds Jordan standing at the sink. She stands there admiring the way his body fills out his jeans.

Alexis tells herself that she has to get a grip on things. She cannot afford to fall in love with Jordan because she is there for other reasons.

Alexis clears her throat startling Jordan.

"Oh, I didn't hear you come in."

"I'm sorry I didn't mean to sneak up on you."

"That's okay my mind is miles away. I was just preparing dinner; I have enough if you care to join me."

"Thanks, but once I finish here I have some others things to take care of."

Jordan glances out of the corner of his eye at Alexis. She seems to be angry about something. He wonders if he has said something to offend her. "Are you okay Alexis? Did I say something to offend you?"

"No, I just had a bad day."

"Would you like to talk about it?"

"No, it's nothing. It will pass." Alexis wants to get far away from Jordan as possible. She doesn't know if she can go through with this, but she doesn't want to disappoint her brother.

Alexis started her work on the main level where Jordan's office is. What she needs is in there but how is she going to get in there to get to his computer without him seeing her. The door to his office is locked but that is not the problem. She had learned from her brother as a child how to pick any lock.

She decides to head up stairs to finish. She knows she has plenty of time to get what she needs. Jordan is on vacation this week so next week she will come in a little earlier while he is at work in order to get into his office and onto his computer.

It takes Alexis three and a half hours to finish cleaning. By the time she finishes, she finds Jordan in his office on the phone.

"Matthew, can you hold on for a minute?" Are you finished already?"

"Yes, everything has been cleaned. If there's nothing else, I should get going."

Jordan walks Alexis to the door and waits until she is safely in her car.

"I'm sorry Matt. That was my new housekeeper."

"Oh, I see you took Mom's advice and hired one."

"Yes, I decided to hire someone to come in three days a week to keep Mom quiet for a while. Next, she will be telling me that I need to marry and give her some grandchildren."

Matthew laughs, "Well, she always thought you would be the first to marry and have a least three kids by now."

"How could I forget that?"

"So how are things going with Jasmine?"

This is something Jordan did not want to talk about with anyone.

"Everything is cool; she stopped by the office this morning. I showed her around the office and Thomas sat her up for her training this week. She starts tomorrow."

Matthew knows Jordan was trying to hide how he feels about Jasmine. He hopes his brother will not let another opportunity pass him by.

"Now back to what you were saying." She breaks into their home and destroys their furniture."

Matthew was giving Jordan the 411 on Brenda. "Man her prints were on everything; the broken glass, the door knob, the knife and even the lipstick tube she left behind.

I was able to get an arrest warrant for her, but when I showed up at her mom's, she has not seen Brenda in a couple of days. Her mom expressed her concern for Brenda. She wants her to get the help that she needs. I have a bad feeling that something bad is about to happen. I just hope I get to her before it does."

"Have you spoken to Donnie and Danielle about your concerns?"

"Yes, I have I told them to keep their eye open for anything or anyone that looks suspicious. You never know with her she could disguise herself as some else."

"You never know with a woman like that. I would not put anything pass her," Jordan comments.

Denise Hill

CHAPTER 24

The next morning, Jasmine wakes early. She stretches and yawns as she gets out of bed. She looks out of her bedroom window and stands there for a minute as she watches the snowfall.

Thirty-five minutes later, Jasmine has showered, dressed and is on her way out the door when her phone rings. She glances at her watch. She has thirty minutes to get to work and she decides to let the answering machine pick up the call.

When Jasmine makes it to her office she finds Thomas standing there waiting.

"Good morning, Jasmine."

"Good morning."

"I have everything set up on your computer," he says as he follows her inside. "I sat your training manuals on the other side of your computer, but before you get started, I would like to introduce you to your fellow coworkers."

After Meeting her coworkers, Jasmine knows this is the place for her. For years she has hoped and prayed for an opportunity like this and to know if was here all along waiting on her return. The warm welcome that she receives from her co-workers was overwhelming. She feels the sincerity in their voices welcoming her to their family. Thomas has been so helpful to her she decides that no matter what the issues are between Jordan and Thomas, she will not let that affect her working relationship with Thomas. She will remain mutual to both of them.

Ronnie stands outside of his office as Jasmine approaches. "Good morning Ronnie," Jasmine says.

"Good morning and welcome aboard. I know Jordan is out this week so if you need anything just let me know."

"I will. Thanks."

Jasmine has just completed four hours of training when Roberto knocks at her door.

"How's it going?"

"Oh my God, I can't believe this training. I hope this week goes by pretty fast."

Roberto smiles, "It will be over before you know it. What I stopped by for is to invite you to lunch if you do not have any plans."

"No, I don't I haven't even thought about lunch."

"Would you like to go?"

"Sure, I could use a break." "Where are we going?"

"It all depends on what you have a taste for."

"I have been craving for a big juicy cheeseburger for days."

"Well I know the perfect place. It's called The Webber Grill."

"Lead the way," Jasmine says.

Roberto and Jasmine head out the building and walk over to the Webber Grill. When they arrive, it is packed. "If I had known we were coming, I could have called and made reservations for us," Roberto says.

Twenty minutes later, the waiter escorted them to their table where he hands them their menus.

"Everything sounds so good, but I think I'll have the Webber Classic and a Pepsi," Jasmine says.

"I'll have the same," Roberto tells the waiter.

Jordan is the focus of their conversation. Jasmine wonders why Roberto is so interested in Jordan's personal life. It was question after question. She begins to wonder if Roberto only asked her to lunch to find out information about Jordan.

Roberto notices the uneasiness with Jasmine as he interrogates her about Jordan and decides to gear the conversation around her.

It is not that Jasmine did not want to talk about Jordan, she could talk about him all day but she made a decision that she would not allow herself to be consumed with Jordan. She has been rejected by him once and did not plan to be rejected again. She knows if they come together, it will be his call.

After lunch, Jasmine heads back to her office to resume the four remaining hours of her training. She stares at the computer screen so long that her eyes feel like they were crossing. She pushes herself away from the computer, walks over to the window, and sits on the ledge. She wonders how much more of this she can take when she remembers Thomas telling her that today would be her longest day of training.

"Thank God for that," she says aloud.

Jordan pulls into his driveway, gets out and heads for the front door. Jordan had driven around for an hour trying to get his thoughts together. He was angry and jealous that Jasmine had gone to lunch with Roberto. Jordan feels very possessive when it comes to Jasmine. He would do anything for her. He would give her the world if she asked for it, but he could not for some reason give her his love.

As Jordan walks inside, his cell phone rings. It is Ronnie.

"Hey, I just wanted to let you know that I went by Toni Reynolds house today. There was a car parked in the driveway so I figured she was there but when I knocked, I did not get an answer. I even sat in my car parked down the street to see if anyone came out. I also received a call from Mr. Jones from the banking center. He said Toni has not shown up for work in a couple of days."

"Do you think she is on to you?" "I doubt it. Mr. Jones says that no one knows she is being investigated but us."

"So are we at a dead end?" Jordan asks.

"No, not really. I still have to view the video tape when it comes in. I should have that by Monday."

"I hope so."

"Are you still salty about Roberto taking Jasmine to lunch?"

"Of course not and who said I was salty anyway"

Ronnie chuckles, "You know you may fool some people, but you will never fool me Jordan. I know you so well. Why don't you make your move and make yourself and Jasmine happy. I swear if you mess this up I will whip your ass myself."

"Are you finished?" Jordan asks.

"Yeah, for now but you know I am going to continue to hound you until you do what is right."

After the conversation with Ronnie, Jordan phones Jasmine at work. Her phone rings a few times before going into voicemail.

Four o'clock finally rolls around. Jasmine has just finished the last of her training for today. She shuts the computer off, stretches back in her chair where she sits for a few minutes with her eyes close trying to relax her eyes until Roberto knocks at her door.

"Are you okay?"

"Yes, I'm okay I was just resting my eyes."

"I was heading out and thought I could walk you to your car if you are ready to leave."

"Oh, you do not have to do that."

"I know."

Jasmine grabs her coat and her purse and walks with Roberto to the elevator.

Ronnie catches a glimpse of the two passing by his office and shakes his head. He knows Jordan had better make his move and quick or Roberto would sweep Jasmine off her feet. He only hoped Jordan knows what he is doing.

CHAPTER 25

Jasmine pulls into her reserve parking space in front of her apartment without noticing she has been followed home. She makes her way halfway to her front door when she glances over her shoulders just in time to see a car speed off. She thinks nothing of it and continues to make her way to her front door. She inserts her key and turns the knob just as her phone rings. Jasmine tosses her coat and purse on the couch and kicks her shoes off before answering the phone.

"Hello."

"Hey there, how did your first day go?" Jordan asks.

"Let's just say that I will be glad when this week is over."

Jordan laughed loudly. He has heard from so many of his employees about training being too long.

"Trust me, it gets shorter each day."

"I know. That's what everyone keeps assuring me of."

"I stopped by the office today to invite you to lunch but I guess Roberto beat me to it," Jordan says sarcastically.

"You should have called me earlier."

"I wanted it to be a surprise, but instead, I wish surprised.

"I'm sorry I feel bad that you came all the way downtown for nothing."

"I had to come down there anyway so it was not a big deal. What are you doing on Saturday?"

"Roberto is stopping by to take a look at my computer for me."

"What's wrong with your computer?"

"I had some files saved on my computer but for some reason I cannot pull them up anymore I think I may have lost them."

"Oh I see. You should have told me, I could have stopped by to take a look at it."

Jasmine can tell that Jordan did not like the idea of Roberto coming over but Jordan is not her man and from the looks of things probably never will be her man so who is he to get upset if she invites someone over.

"Well the next time I have any problems with my computer Jordan, you will be the first person I call."

"I know you just got home so I will let you get yourself settled and I will phone you later, maybe we can get together sometime this week and do something."

"Okay that sounds like a plan," Jasmine says.

~ ccxxviii ~

Worn down from the week of hell, Danielle wants a hot bath to relax.

Donnie prepares dinner so that she can wine down and relax. She has been working her ass off since her boss fired Brenda, but luckily, they have found a replacement for Brenda today.

It has been two weeks since anyone has heard or seen Brenda. Danielle has been on pins and needles she feels Brenda will try something again eventually.

Jasmine has convinced Danielle to join the fitness center with her to help relieve some of the stress she is under. Unfortunately, it only makes Danielle feel worse. She feels more out of shape than ever. Her whole body aches. Her body feels as though she has been hit with a Mac truck. This morning when she climbed out of bed, she could barely move her legs.

Danielle had joined the fitness center on Monday. She swore if her body continues to feel this way, she would have to disappoint Jasmine and quit.

Danielle is only thirty-two but today she feels more like sixty-two.

Danielle sits in the tub with a glass of wine relaxing as she listens to Dave Koz. She is thankful that today is Friday. She hopes that tomorrow her body will be relieved of the aches and pains that she has felt over the week. Saturday was the day that she and her husband have made plans to go Christmas shopping for the boys.

Donnie and the boys have finished dinner. The boys go to their room to play their video games while Donnie decides to check on his wife.

Donnie knocks at the bathroom door a couple of times before entering. He stands at the door looking at the women who he loves more than life itself, as she lay asleep in the tub. He thinks how he almost lost her over his careless mistake with their houseguest.

Donnie walks over to the tub and kneels down on both knees. He reaches into the water for Danielle's hand and holds it in his. He raises her hand to his mouth and kisses her hand gently.

Danielle opens her eyes and smiles. She loves Donnie with all her heart. It is hard for her to think that she almost had an affair with a co-worker who she knows was not the man that Donnie is. She realizes that they both have made mistakes that have taught them both about true love. True love is hard to find and when you find it, you have better hold on to it for dear life. If not, there will always be someone waiting around to take it from you.

Over the weeks, Jasmine and Roberto have become close. In no way was Jasmine attractive to Roberto as everyone around them think. He was just a friend, a male companion who she relies on to escort her places when she does not want to go alone.

~ CCXXX ~

Although Jordan does not approve of their relationship, he never tells Jasmine how he feels about her or the relationship that she has with Roberto.

Jasmine has been working for Jordan for two weeks. Their relationship is strictly business but Jasmine wants more, but there was no way she would allow herself to be rejected by him. Jasmine knows Jordan does not like the fact that she and Roberto were close but then again he is not her man. Jasmine has developed an attitude that she could care less about what Jordan likes or dislikes. Ever since she walked in his office and found Vanessa there discussing the charity ball with him, it did something to her that she could not explain. Jasmine became distant with Jordan. She only speaks with him when needed and tries to avoid him at all cost.

Later she learns that Jordan and Vanessa are Co-Chairman of the board for the battered women shelter and that every year they hold a ball to raise money for that charity.

Jordan notices over the weeks that Jasmine has had very little to say especially to him and he wants to find out what was going on with her. After all, he loves this woman and wants her to be his but in his time.

Jordan calls Jasmine into his office. "Can you shut the door behind you," he says.

Jasmine took the empty seat in front of Jordan's desk. She is nervous and she tries to avoid eye contact with him. She is afraid that he will see the hurt and sadness in her eyes and the last thing that she wants from him is pity.

"Would you care to tell me what's going on with you?"

"What are you talking about Jordan?"

"Come on Jasmine, you're not stupid and neither am I." "You chit chat with everyone around here but when it comes to me, it's like you try to avoid me. Have I done something to offend you?"

Jasmine thinks about how she can respond without telling Jordan the truth, the fact that she wants him more than ever and that seeing Vanessa here in his office alone with him made her angry. "I'm sorry Jordan, but I don't know how to respond to that question. You are my boss and the way I act and treat my co-workers will always be different from the way I treat you."

"So just because I'm the boss, you can't be yourself around me. You try to avoid me as much as possible. Is that it?"

Jasmine is furious by this time. She cannot believe that by her not wanting to have any contact with Jordan has gotten her called into his office. "Jordan do you really want the truth? Are you sure you can handle the truth?" Jasmine says so loud that anyone standing outside of Jordan's office can hear.

Ronnie just happens to be standing outside his office and can hear the two.

Hearing Jasmine raise her voice, Jordan knows he has hit a nerve.

"I love you Jordan and have always loved you from the moment I laid eyes on you, but you continue to play these little games with me. One minute I think you are feeling me, and the next minute it is strictly business with you. I moved back to Indianapolis so that I can be closer to my family and to be close to you and if you do not want me, honey there are plenty of men out here that do." Jasmine stands up and heads for the door when Jordan rushes from behind his desk and cuts her off.

Jordan eases Jasmine up against the door. "Is this what you want," Jordan asks as he kisses Jasmine on the lips. Jasmine opens her mouth and Jordan enters. He kisses her as he has never done before. He wants her just as much as she wants him. Jasmine can feel Jordan as rubs up against her. The thought of him inside her drives her wild. Jasmine rubs her hand along the length of him as she unzips his pants and removes him from his boxers. She bends to her knees and takes him in her mouth. She runs her tongue along the tip and up and down the side of him before taking all of him back into her mouth. The feel of Jasmines mouth wrapped around him causes him to moan.

Jordan stands back and eases Jasmines up where he slides his hand under her skirt and pulls down her stockings along with her thong. He parts the lips of her womanhood and strokes her bud until Jasmine cannot stand it anymore. Jordan

lifts Jasmine in his arms and carries her over to the couch where he lays her down.

Jordan kicks off his shoes unbuttons his belt. Jasmine lays there in awe she cannot

believe the man she loves is undressing before her in his office. In less than a

minute, Jordan is undressed he lowers his body on top of hers he begins to kiss her

wildly his hands goes under her shirt. He raises her bra as he brings his mouth to

her breast. He takes one of her breast into his mouth as his other hand caresses the

other. Jordan brings his mouth back to hers and they kiss as if it were their last

kiss. Jordan parts her legs with his and enters her slowly. He begins to stoke her

slowly her body began to move in motion with his.

"Oh Jasmine, I have wanted this forever. I love you with all my heart", Jordan

says as he goes deeper and deeper into Jasmine.

"Oh Jordan baby this feels so damn good," Jasmine says.

"I'm about to come I want you to come with me," Jordan says.

"I'm with you baby all the way."

They two come together and it is something that they have never experience

with anyone. They laid there without speaking for a minute. "I'm sorry Jasmine, I

didn't protect you." Jasmine did not respond, she thinks about how things would

be if Jordan gets her pregnant.

Jordan stands up as Jasmine continues to lie he kneels down to her. "I'm sorry Jasmine but I could not help myself. I wanted our first time to be special."

Jasmine looks at Jordan with love in her eyes, "It was special to me Jordan."

CHAPTER 26

Ronnie is standing in the hall and hears the commotion between Jordan and Jasmine. He is a little irritated with Jordan. He knows how Jordan feels about Jasmine and cannot understand why this man is taking his time to make a move with her. He phones Jordan's office when everything goes quiet and when Jordan does not answer, he can only guess as to why. "That's my boy!" Ronnie shouts.

An hour later, Jordan is working away at his desk when he looks up to find Ronnie standing at his door with a smile plastered to his face.

"What's up with you?" Jordan asks.

"I think I should be asking you that. Oh, the smell of sex is still in the air," Ronnie jokes.

"Come in and shut my door," Jordan says. "Now what are you taking about."

"Oh you know damn well what I am talking about and it's about time." Jordan cannot hide the smile that is threatening to appear.

"I feel bad I did not protect her and that our first time was here in my office. I have never made love to anyone in my office. I am strictly about business when it comes to the office. I should have had more control but when it comes to her I have no control."

"Well, don't go beating yourself up over this. Sometimes the lovemaking is better when you do it in a not so natural place. And if nothing else, she will always remember it happen here first."

"You are nuts; I do not know how Sheila puts up with you."

"I'm glad it was me standing out in the hall to hear you guys instead of Roberto," Ronnie laughs as he shakes his head.

"Yeah, that's another thing that I will have to take care of because that shit that's going on between them will stop. I will not allow another man to take my time with my woman from me."

"Oh so you guys have made it official?"

"No, not yet but we will eventually." Ronnie shakes his head. "Jordan what the hell is wrong with you?"

"I don't want to rush it with her."

"Well I would say that you are too late for that. Don't be surprise when you finally decide to go to her and Roberto has beaten you to her."

"Why do you think he is trying to manipulate all of her time?"

"Don't worry I know what I'm doing. After today, she will not think about anyone else."

~ ccxxxviii ~

"Oh so you put it down like that? Um, I hope you are right."

"I don't to mean to change the subject, but how are things coming along with the investigation?"

"Not good." "It looks as though Toni Reynolds has disappeared and now there is a problem with the video tape that came back. The company sent the wrong video and now they are having problem locating the right one. They think they could have possibly erased it or taped over it."

"That's some bullshit." "I know for a fact that those tapes cannot be erased or taped over. They keep them for seven years and then destroyed because once they are used they cannot do anything with the tapes afterward but store them for instances like this."

"Calm down Jordan, I have an appointment with a guy who runs the central location on Thursday." "You're welcome to come along if you like."

"I would love to but I need to work on getting things together for the Christmas party."

This year Jordan wants to host the Christmas party that he gives every year for his staff at his home. He usually rents out one of the ballrooms at the Madame Walker Theater but this year he wants this it to be different. He has hired a party planner who will take care of all the planning. She has hired a caterer and on Thursday, he is going over there to do a little food tasting. He wants to taste the food beforehand.

Later that evening Jasmine makes it home after a hard workout with Danielle. The workout is what she needs after the lovemaking that she shared with Jordan. She has told Danielle about what had happened in Jordan's office. Danielle laughs so hard that she falls off the treadmill. "I cannot believe that Jordan would make love to anyone at the office, but I guess you were just too much for him today." They both laughed.

"Oh my God Danielle, I did not want to feel for Jordan what I am feeling right now because I'm afraid that this will lead to another rejection and right now I don't think I can handle that."

"You need to sit down and talk with him about it and let him know if nothing will become of the two of you that you would rather keep everything strictly business. He can only abide by your wishes but I think you have Jordan all wrong. Like I said, this is so not like Jordan to do what he did today, that should tell you something."

An hour later Jasmine runs her bath water. She wants to soak her body because she feels the soreness from today's activity with Jordan. She goes into her bedroom where she undresses. She pulls a nightshirt and a pair of panties from the dresser drawer and lays them across the bed.

Jasmine relaxes in the tub as the soft sound of Paul Taylor echoes throughout the bathroom.

~ ccxl ~

Jasmine has been in the tub for about an hour and has dozed off when the sound of something falling to the ground wakes her. She grabs her towel and eases out of the tub. She walks down the hall to the kitchen where she sees the picture that hangs on the wall has fallen to the ground shattering the glass.

Jasmine walks back to her bedroom to get dress so that she can clean the glass up but when she goes back to her room, she is speechless. The nightshirt that she had laid out has been replaced with a red teddy.

Jasmine knows she does not own a red teddy so where did this come from she wonders. Jasmine picks up the teddy when she sees that someone had ejaculated on the teddy in the crouch area. All sorts of thoughts begin to race through her mind. Is someone still in the apartment she thinks when all of a sudden she hears knocking at her front door? Jasmine rushes to the door and opens it without checking to see who is out there.

Jordan stands looking at Jasmine who has a look of terror on her face.

Jordan grabs her into his arms, "What's the matter Jordan asks?"

"I think someone has been in my apartment while I was in the bath tub."

"What?" Stay right here," Jordan says as he searches her apartment. They only thing that he found was the picture and the broken glass. He also notices that her patio door had been slightly opened. Jordan walks back to where Jasmine is.

"Did you leave your patio door open?"

"No, it was locked."

Jordan pulls out his phone and calls the police.

Jasmine walks into her bedroom with Jordan to let him see the teddy. "This does not belong to me. I laid across my bed a nightshirt and a pair of my panties which are now gone. Look at what someone has done to this teddy." Jordan has an eerie feeling about this. "I do not feel comfortable with you staying here alone tonight. I want you to pack an overnight bag you can stay in one of my guest bedrooms for the night. Now go ahead and get dress before the police arrive."

Jordan pace back and forth in the living room until the police arrives. When the police arrive, they search the apartment and find fingerprints that are on the patio door handle. They bag the teddy as evidence but both officers know without a suspect, the DNA results will be useless.

One of the officers hands Jasmine a card and tells her to call if anything unusual happens or if she remembers anything that will be helpful to them in catching this person. They also tell her to have the maintenance people come over and replace the lock on her patio door. Although she thinks she had been locking her patio door, someone has deliberately broken apiece preventing it from locking.

Denise Hill

CHAPTER 27

Jordan and Jasmine arrive at his place a little after eight. Jasmine pulls in behind Jordan. As they enter his home, Jasmine turns to Jordan and asks, "So are you going to give me a tour of your home this time?"

"I'll give you whatever it is you want, but first, I want you to call your parents and let them know what has happen and that you will be staying here with me."

Jordan leads Jasmine down the hall to the phone on the wall.

"I'll take your things up to your room and then I will show you around."

After the tour of his home, Jasmine is very impressed. Jordan begins to explain to her why he lives in such a large home when it is just him.

"When I was younger, my dad took me to one of his company's barbeque which was at his boss's home. I fell in love with his house. It was humongous and from that day forward I make a promise that someday I would have a house just as big and beautiful as his. I worked hard to get where I am today. I think that is what some of our young people today lack. They don't have someone to show him or her that if they work hard and stay out of trouble that they can experience the things that I have and accomplished anything they want to. They don't have to become a rapper or athlete to be successful. I know when I was young I would tell some of my friends that I was going to be very rich and successful. They all laughed but today I have the last laugh. You know there is so much negativity out there amongst our black people. Some of them hate to see another brother or sister get ahead and then they start to hate. That is the one reason I joined Big Brothers is to give young boys guidance that they may not be getting at home. I help them with their studies. I introduce them to things that they would otherwise not know exist."

"Jordan I think that is wonderful that you take time out of your busy schedule to do things for our young black men. Most men do not have time or they feel that it is not their responsibility to help guide them through life. You should be commended for that."

"I have been commended with my success."

The last room that Jordan shows Jasmine is the room that she will occupy. Jasmine is a little disappointed at first to learn that she and Jordan will actually have separate rooms but is glad that she does not have to spend the night alone in her apartment.

Jordan opens the door to her room. He has placed her overnight bag on the large king size bed.

"I will leave you to get settled. If you need anything, just let me know."

As Jasmine enters the room, she is astonished at the size. The guest room is almost the size of her apartment. Inside the cozy room was a King size sleigh bed. To her left was a sitting area with an electric cherry wood fireplace. The bathroom was bigger than her bedroom, and contains a full size walk - in closet, a Jacuzzi tub and his and her sink.

Jasmine walks over to the fireplace and flips the switch. The fireplace lights up and the sound of soft jazz echoes throughout the room.

Jasmine walks over to open the French doors that lead to the balcony. The balcony overlooks the lake. The view alone is breath taking. Jasmine steps out onto the balcony, the breeze from the cool night air hits her she inhales a deep breath as she stands alone taking in all the events that has gone down today. This is not how her life is supposed to be. She wants to be here with Jordan but under different circumstances.

Jordan walks down the hall to his bedroom. He opens the French doors that led to his balcony and steps outside. In the summer, Jordan spends many of his nights sitting on his balcony relaxing with a drink or two listening to some jazz.

Jordan stands quietly on his balcony as he fights for control of both his body and mind as he watches Jasmine from a distance. He loves this woman more than life itself and cannot bring himself to tell her how he really feels about her. He cannot tell her how happy he feels having her near him.

Jordan finally steps into the moonlight to reveal his appearance. "It is a beautiful night isn't it?" Jordan says as he startles Jasmine.

"Oh my God Jordan, you scared me!"

"I'm sorry I didn't intend to."

Oh, by the way, I took the liberty of ordering dinner. I hope that's okay."

"Yes, I am starved."

"Well when you are ready, come on down to the kitchen."

Jordan walks back into his room and heads downstairs to the kitchen. He gets himself a beer and stands looking out of his kitchen window as he sips on his Budweiser. Jordan is fighting a battle with himself by doing the right thing by Jasmine. He wants so badly for her to share his bed and make passionate love to her every night but he knows this is not the right thing to do until he can fully commit himself to her. He needs to avoid any sexual contact with her as much as possible.

After dinner had been delivered, Jordan marches his way upstairs to get Jasmine. Jordan knocks at the door a couple of times before entering. As he enters, he is unable to move, Jasmine is laid out across the bed in her nightshirt. The first thought that comes to his mind is to slip out of his clothes and join Jasmine in bed. The nightshirt stops at her rear end exposing her shapely golden brown thighs. At this moment memories of their first time clouded his mind, an electrifying shutter runs through his body that lingers at his manhood.

Jordan licks his lips as he moves closer to the bed. He leans down to brush his fingers through her hair. Jordan calls out to her, his voice low and husky. Jasmine opens her eyes as she meets his gaze. She smiles a warm smile as she sits up in the bed.

"I'm sorry to have wakened you but I wanted to come and get you for dinner."

"That's okay because I am starved. By the way this room is out of this world."

Jordan smiles. "I'm glad you like it."

Jordan sits down on the bed trying to hide the bulge in his pants.

"Is something wrong Jordan?" Jasmine asks.

"No, everything is fine. Why don't you come down when you are ready?"

Jordan makes his escape back to the kitchen. "Man this is going to be harder than I thought," he says aloud.

After dinner, Jordan and Jasmine move to the family room where they sit by the fire flirting openly with each other. Jordan is thankful for the company. He has spent so many lonely nights in his home wondering what he has done for so many of his relationships to always end the same way. He had given the women he had been involved with everything they could ask for but that did not seem to be enough.

"Well Jordan, let me tell you this. If a woman is truly in love with you, it doesn't matter that you give them expensive gifts or take them to the nicest places if you are not giving yourself to them. You need to learn to loosen up and live a little, take chances. I bet today was the first time that you have ever had sex in your office." "Am I right?"

Jordan cannot say anything but nod.

"Jordan, I guarantee you things will be different in your next relationship."

Jasmine makes Jordan look at things in a different prospective. She makes him want to do things that he would not normally do. He feels comfortable being himself around her.

At the end of the night, the two have come to an agreement that they would not make love with us other until he can give her what she really wants, which is all of him.

Over the next two weeks, the living arrangement is taking a toll on Jordan and Jasmine. The flirtation between them is something more and Jasmine is hungry for it. She has made an agreement with Jordan about them not making love, but she is determined to make him just as miserably as she is. She purposely walks around in the morning in the skimpiest night clothes she can find to torture him and he knows it.

"Two can play this game," Jordan thinks.

The next morning Jordan comes down to breakfast in nothing more than his underwear. His underwear leaves nothing to the imagination.

As Jasmine turns the corner to the kitchen, she stops in her tracks. She struggles to maintain some self-control as she watches Jordan from behind. The view is enough to make her forget about their agreement.

Jordan turns just in time to see the look of lust in her eyes. Jordan walks over to Jasmine and whispers into her ear, allowing his full lips to brush like a whisper against the line of her flesh. "Good morning sweetheart."

It gives him great pleasure to give her a little taste of her own medicine.

Jordan takes a seat at the table and smiles.

"Now you know what it feels like," he says to himself. The two sit in silence eating breakfast. Both infuriated with each other.

Jasmine glances up at Jordan. "Oh he gets on my last nerve," she says to herself.

Jordan keeps his head down as he curses himself for allowing her to get the best of him.

~ ccl ~

The night before, Jordan lay awake in bed listening to water from the shower coming from the guest bedroom. He pictured her brown skin covered in soap as he imagined himself washing her down from head to toe. Unable to take anymore he stepped out on to his balcony to cool off.

The nights are harder for him than any other time, but he knows in time things would eventually turn out the way he wanted but in the meantime, he had to learn to control himself when it comes to Jasmine.

CHAPTER 28

The next morning Jasmine leaves the house frustrated and to make matters worse, when she arrive to her parking spot, Vanessa is parked next to her leaning against her car. Vanessa waits as Jasmine gets out of her car and walks over to confront her.

"I am not in the mood for this," Jasmine says.

Jasmine walks pass Vanessa heading for the elevator when Vanessa calls out to her.

"Jasmine, can I have a word with you?"

"What is it Vanessa? I do not have time for any of your bullshit this morning."

"I've been hearing rumors about you moving into Jordan's home."

"What does that have anything to do with you?"

"Let me just make myself clear," Vanessa says as she walks closer to Jasmine.

"You may have him now but remember he will always love me. What we have is special and I doubt that any other woman will ever experience what we shared. It will be hard for Jordan to give himself to the next woman because I still have his heart. You will always come in second to me bitch, especially since I am carrying his child!"

"If you cared so much for Jordan then why did you sleep with his employee? You are one of those women who want their cake and ice cream to, but guess what, I have Jordan now and no matter how hard you try, you will not be able to tear us apart, not even with your claim of carrying his baby. So pump your brakes bitch and leave us alone," Jasmine says as she gets into the parking garage's elevator.

Jasmine rides the elevator in silence. How can she deny what Vanessa has said when she feels in her heart that Jordan is still in love with Vanessa and now she is claiming to be carrying his child. "How can I compete with that?" She thinks to herself.

For the rest of the day, Jasmine avoids Jordan as much as possible. She constantly thinks about what Vanessa has said and concludes that this is the reason he cannot fully commit himself to her. He is still in love with Vanessa.

When Jasmine arrives home, Jordan is already there. As she makes her way inside, Jordan is in the kitchen. Once he hears the front door open, he comes out to greet her with a kiss. Jordan holds her in his arms and bends down to get a taste of her luscious lip but Jasmine turns just in time and his kiss lands on her cheek. Jordan takes a step back, "Are you okay? "Did I do something wrong?"

"No, I'm just tired and have a splitting headache." She lied for she was deeply saddened to think that Vanessa still holds Jordan's heart and the fact that she is carrying his child, which he has not mention to her.

"Why don't you go up and take your bath and relax. Check your medicine cabinet. I think there may be some Tylenol in there if not, look in mine. I will come up and get you when dinner is ready.

Jasmine smiles a weak smile and makes her way upstairs.

Jordan watches as Jasmine climbs the stairs. He stands wondering what is bothering Jasmine before heading back to the kitchen.

When Jordan is finished with dinner, he decides to call Jasmine on the intercom.

By the time Jasmine comes down, Jordan is on his second helping. "I thought I was going to have to come up and get you," Jordan says as he smiles at Jasmine.

"I sorry, I just need to clear my head a little before I came down."

"Is there something bothering you?" Jordan asks with a concerned look. He knows Vanessa had dropped by the office this morning and he had only hoped that Jasmine and Vanessa did not run into each other.

The two eat in silence until Jordan cannot take it anymore. "You seem to be very busy today or were you avoiding me?"

"I guess it was a little of both," Jasmine says without making eye contact with Jordan.

Jordan stops eating and sits there observing Jasmine. Just then, Jasmine feels nauseated and light headed. She pushes herself away from the table and rushes to the bathroom. Jasmine has been feeling a little queasy today and just figured it was something that she had for lunch. When she returns to the kitchen, Jordan is gone. He is disappointed when learning that Jasmine had deliberately avoided him at work today.

Jasmine picks up the plate with her unfinished dinner, walks over to the garbage disposal, and empties the remainder of her dinner into the sink before placing the dish in the dishwasher. Still feeling a little queasy. Jasmine opens the refrigerator and removes a can of 7up; this seems to have always worked when she was a kid.

Jasmine goes down the hall to the family room where she finds Jordan unraveling the Christmas lights.

"You need some help?"

Jordan looks up. "Sure if you can stand to be around me."

Jasmine makes no comment as she moves further into the room. She picks up another pair of lights and starts to untangle them.

They work in silence until they hear the sound of the doorbell. Jasmine looks up at Jordan with a look that says let me guess who that could be.

Jordan makes his way to the door and when he opens the door, he finds Vanessa on his steps. Jasmine can hear Vanessa voice questioning him about his morals which is a joke.

~ cclvi ~

"I can't believe you would move her in your home." "How long have you been fucking her Jordan?"

"Vanessa, what I do and who I do it with is none of your business. Just like whom you do it with is none of mine."

Vanessa pushes pass Jordan and walks into the family room. "Well, isn't this cozy?" "The two of you are getting ready to decorate the tree and sit by the fireplace." Jasmine glances in Vanessa's direction and continues to do what she was doing. She is afraid that if she speaks she will lay into Vanessa something terrible.

Vanessa walks closer to Jasmine without saying a word. Jordan rush to stand in the middle of the two. He has no idea what is going to jump off but he wants to be close just in case.

By this time, Jasmine is fuming. She steps in front of Jordan placing herself directly in front of Vanessa and begins to point her finger in her face. "I don't know what your problem is but I damn sure can solve it for you."

"You know damn well what my problem is, you bitch," Vanessa yells as she moves closer to Jasmine.

Jasmine takes a step back. "If I knew what your problem was believe me I would solve it real quick and as far as me being a bitch, I'll be your bitch but just know I am a good bitch and that's why I am living here and you are not. Just know that the next time you call me out of my name, I will show you how bad of a bitch I am."

Vanessa sneers, "You don't want any of this Jasmine, trust me."

"Keeping trying me Vanessa and you will find out firsthand what I do to bitches who think they are all that."

Having heard enough of the nonsense, Jordan orders Vanessa to leave. He grabs her by the arm and escorts her to the front door.

Jasmine smiles at Vanessa just to rub it in a little deeper but on the inside she is furious with Jordan. She cannot understand why he would even allow her in his home. Jasmine has had enough of the whole Jordan thing. She decides that if this relationship is to be it will happen but right now, she knows returning to her apartment is what she needs to do.

Jasmine stands looking out of the window as Jordan and Vanessa argued outside. "This man has got to be the biggest fool for that woman to let her get to him the way she does. I need to take myself out of the picture to see if what they shared is really that special, if it's not, then Vanessa better back the hell up because I won't give up so easily the next time."

When Jordan finally comes back inside, he stands in the entryway of the family room. It is empty. He does not blame Jasmine if she never wants to see him again.

~ cclviii ~

He cannot believe that he allowed Vanessa in his home again. He remembered the last time she was here. She had confronted his housekeeper and accused him of breaking up with her for Alexis who was young enough to be his daughter.

He knows he had better get his head together or he will end up without Jasmine a second time.

Jordan climbs the stairs to the fourth floor and takes a seat on the top step. He does not know what to say to Jasmine about what has just happened. He learned from Vanessa that she had bumped into Jasmine this morning and told her that bullshit about her still having his heart. He had to be honest with himself and Jasmine. He knows deep inside that Vanessa still has a part of his heart, but it was Jasmine, who he wants to spend the rest of his life with, and that someday Jasmine will have his whole heart, but right now, he has to get over Vanessa completely before he can allow himself to enjoy Jasmine. His biggest fear is if Jasmine knows how he feels, he will lose her for good.

CHAPTER 29

Jasmine has been planning to return to her apartment. Being around Jordan and not being able to have him the way she wants him is just too much for her. She can deal with working with him but living under the same roof is a little too much for her and especially since she knows Vanessa still holds a part of his heart and is carrying his child.

Jasmine is upstairs packing her belongings. She feels this is a good time as any to get this out of the way. She has only been there for a short period but in that time, she has become attached to the home. As she glances around the room, it looks as if it has been designed especially for her.

Jasmine looks up to find Jordan standing in the doorway. "Hey, what's up?" Jasmine asks.

"Are you sure this is what you want?" Jordan asks.

"To be honest Jordan, no, this is not what I want. It's what I know has to be done. You have no idea how hard this is for me to lie awake in bed knowing that you are alone in the next room. There have been so many nights that I wanted to come to you and I could not."

Jordan brings his hands to touch her face. "Sweetheart, do you think it has been easy for me?" "You walk around here teasing me in the skimpiest things you call pajamas and you don't think that's hard on me?"

"That's why I have to do what I have to do. I don't want to end up hating you Jordan."

Jordan walks over and grabs a hold of her hand. Jasmine takes a step backwards; the electrifying touch is too much for her to bear. Just then she gets queasy, she feels as if she is about to vomit and pass out. Jasmine rushes into the bathroom and shut the door behind her. She knows her period is a couple of days late but thinks nothing of it until she continues to get sick every day.

Jordan knocks at the bathroom door, "Jasmine are you okay in there?"

"Yes, I am fine." Jasmine lies. There is no way she is going to tell Jordan what she thinks is causing her sickness.

Jordan sits down on the edge of the bed and waits for Jasmine to come out.

Jordan thinks about the situation as he waits for Jasmine to emerge from the bathroom. He knows he needs to do or say something that will persuade her to stay even if that meant breaking his promise that he has made to her. "I love this woman and have waited for a life time for this. "I can't let her slip through my fingers again," he says to himself.

~ cclxii ~

Jasmine looks in the mirror trying to get herself together as the tears run down her face. If she is pregnant, she knows Jordan will do the right thing by her and the child but what about Vanessa and her child. Whom will he marry? True enough she wants nothing more to be Mrs. Daniels but not like this. She wants Jordan to marry her because he loves her and wants to spend the rest of his life with her not because of the baby.

"God, please don't let me be pregnant," she says as she wipes the tears that continue to fall.

Jasmine finally comes out of the bathroom, her eyes red and puffy from crying. Jordan is confused. He thinks she has gotten sick but from the looks of things, he can tell she has been crying.

Jordan rushes to her side and wraps his arms around her. "Jasmine, please rethink your decision about leaving. I need you here with me."

Those words are like music to her ears but right now, she needs more from him than just words.

Jordan has convinced Jasmine to stay. The rest of the week turns out to be magical for her. Unbelievably, Jordan has given himself to her. On Wednesday evening, Jordan moves her belonging into his room before she arrives home from work.

Jasmine arrives home that evening just as Alexis finishes gathering the information from Jordan's personal computer. Jasmine walks through the door and catches Alexis coming out of Jordan's office.

"Hey Alexis," Jasmine says. Startled Alexis turns around to see Jasmine standing at the door. She wonders how long Jasmine has been standing there and if she has seen her on Jordan's computer.

"I thought Jordan's office was off limits?" Jasmine says.

"It is," Jordan, says as he stands at the top of the stairs.

Alexis is caught red handed. She has already been warned twice about his office being off limits to her.

"Alexis I need to speak with you in private," Jordan says as he comes down the stairs.

"I'll be upstairs in my room if you need me."

Jordan has become leery of Alexis after he has caught her trying to get into his office. He decides that if he cannot trust her, she has no business working in his home.

Alexis left with her final paycheck in hand and three personal bank account numbers that belong to Jordan. She smiles as she makes her way to her car.

"This mother fucker thinks he is hurting me; let's see who will be hurting when his money continues to slips out of his bank accounts."

When Jasmine enters her bedroom and goes to her closet, she is speechless. All of her belongings are gone. She checks the dresser drawers and they are empty as well. Jasmine walks over to the chaise and takes a seat wondering what is going on. Did Jordan reconsider her decision to leave? All kinds of thoughts clouded her head until she hears a knock at the door.

"Come in." Jordan sticks his head in, "I forgot to tell you that I moved all of your belongings into my room where they belong."

Jasmine smiles, "I thought you changed your mind about me staying."

Jordan moves further into the room and Jasmine goes rushing into his open arms. Jordan tilts her head up, "Sweetheart, I told you that I love you with all my heart and I plan to show you every day as long as I live."

Jordan kisses her forehead and laughs. "You know that void that was in my life, it's no longer there. Jasmine you make me whole." With no words spoken, Jordan brings his head down and brushes his lips against hers. Jasmine parts her lips and allows him to enter. Jordan scoops her up in his arms, makes his way to their bedroom, and lays her gently across the bed. He kicks his slippers off, removes his tee shirt, and throws it across the room.

Jordan begins to undress Jasmine slowly taking in the beauty of her firm breast and her shapely golden brown thighs until she is completely nude. He gets down on his knees and pulls Jasmines body to the edge of the bed where he parts her legs and slides his tongue up and down her womanhood licking and sucking her womanhood.

Jasmine is in awe. The feeling of Jordan's warm tongue drives her wild. She grabs a hold of his head and pulls him in for dear life.

Jasmine begins to shudder letting her juices flow as Jordan continues to feast on her. "Jordan, I need you inside of me now." Jasmine shouts.

Jordan moves up her body planting little kisses as he makes his way to her breast. He licks her nipple before taking it into his mouth.

"Jordan please, I can't take this any longer, I need you inside of me."

Jordan removes his pants and boxers. He pulls a foil from his pants pocket and slides it onto his pole. He enters Jasmine slowly, with each stroke, he goes deeper and deeper in and out. Jasmine matches his rhythm moaning out his name repeatedly until she cannot contain her orgasm any longer. Jordan follows pursuit and explodes inside of her.

~ cclxvi ~

Denise Hill

CHAPTER 30

Donnie and Danielle's marriage has been better than ever. The thought of losing their family has brought them closer than before. The boys are ecstatic when their dad returns home.

"Wake up sleepy heads." "All dad, I just went to sleep," Donnie Jr. says.

Donnie smiles. His eldest son has never been a morning person and he will always come up with some excuse to sleep in a little longer.

Donnie scoops his sleepy son out of bed and places him on his feet.

"This is your last day for two weeks. Today will be filled with lots of excitement. You have your Christmas party and your gift exchange at school. Now I know you don't want to miss out on that."

"I can't wait to get to school," Derek says.

Donnie drops the boys off at school and is heading to work when he spies Brenda in his rear view mirror.

"What the hell is she doing?" Donnie says to himself.

~ cclxviii ~

Donnie continues to drive until his reaches the FedEx parking lot. He pulls into his reserved space and hops out waving a piece of paper in the air as he approaches Brenda's car.

"Don't you know I have a restraining order against you? You are not allowed within 500 feet of me or my family."

Brenda steps out of the car, "Fuck that piece of paper. Do you honestly believe that piece of paper is going to keep me away from you? You can try and deny it all you want Donnie, but I know you want me," Brenda says as she moves closer to Donnie.

Brenda opens her trench coat to reveal her red lace bra and her red lace thong. "I know you want this so why don't you stop pretending."

Donnie cocks his head to the side trying hard not to notice the firm brown breast and the firm thick thighs that are before him. "You are one sick bitch," Donnie says as he turns and walks toward the entrance of the building.

Before entering, he stops and turns around. "If you are not gone in five minutes, I'm calling the police."

Donnie makes his way to his office and walks over to the window just in time to see Brenda pull off. Donnie continues to stare out of the window as feelings of guilt floors him. The sight of Brenda in the red lace bra brings back memories of that dreadful night. He had lied to his wife and to himself. He had known it was Brenda the whole time but the feeling of his penis in her mouth was breath taking.

The feeling that ran through his body as she licked the top of his head was so overwhelming that there was no way he could have ask her stop and to leave his home. He would just have to suffer the consequences and suffering is what he has done. He feels his manhood raising as he continues to think about that night.

Brenda pulls into her mom's driveway and sits there. She has to prepare herself for one of her mom's lectures. She has not been back since their last argument.

Brenda inserts the key into the lock but before she has a chance to turn the knob, the door is snatched opened.

"Girl!" What have you gotten yourself into this time?" her mom yells.

"Mom please, not now, I just need to rest."

"Rest, you're going to get all the rest you need while you are sitting in jail. I have a good mind to call that detective and have him come right over here and lock your trifling behind up. Why do you keep doing this to yourself messing with these married men? Can't you find a good single man? Oh I forgot you don't like single men you're just like your father always wanting something you can't have."

Brenda turns to look at her mom, "I see why dad left you. You're always bitching about something," Brenda says as she makes her way to the back bedroom where she slams the door shut. She is in no mood to listen to her mom belittle her or her father.

~ cclxx ~

Brenda sits down on the bed with her hands up to her face. She has to find a way to make Donnie see that he needs her.

Brenda lay in the bed for hours thinking of a way to get Danielle out of the picture for good.

Later that evening, Donnie and the boys arrive home ten minutes before Danielle. Donnie has stopped and picked up pizza for boys and Chinese food for Danielle and him. He tells the boys to go wash their hands while he sets the table.

Five minutes later, Danielle walks in with a look of terror on her face. Donnie wonders what is wrong until he sees Brenda behind Danielle with a gun pointed to her back.

"Brenda what the hell are you up to?" Donnie asks as he moves toward them.

"Donnie stop right where you are or I will shoot this bitch in the back."

"Calm down Brenda and put the gun down. You don't want to do anything stupid."

"Stupid, no I was stupid for not doing this a long time ago." "Your wife has caused me so much trouble. You do not know how many nights I lay awake thinking of killing her. She does not deserve you and you know it. I could be a better wife to you. Tell her Donnie," Brenda yells.

Just then, the boys run into the kitchen to see what is going on.

"Go back to your room," Danielle yells.

All eyes are on the boys when Danielle turns around quickly and tries to grab the gun from Brenda. Donnie runs toward them when the gun goes off. Silence fills the room as Donnie grabs his stomach and falls to the floor. Danielle runs to Donnie as Brenda runs out the front door.

"Donnie, Danielle screams. Blood quickly covers the lower part of his shirt. "Oh my God, please Donnie don't you die on me. Just hold on baby," Danielle says as she reaches for her cell phone and dials 911.

Donnie has been in surgery for four hours while his family waits patiently in the waiting room. Danielle is frantic. She feels that this is her fault for allowing Brenda into their lives. Jasmine tries hard to comfort Danielle and to make her see that this is not her fault.

Jordan and Jasmine had been in the middle of dinner when Jordan receives the call that Donnie has been shot. When they arrived, his mom and siblings were with Danielle in the waiting area.

Matthew had taken off shortly after they arrived. He was determined to find Brenda and put her behind bars where she belonged. However, little did he know Brenda has been at the hospital disguised as a nurse waiting on Donnie's recovery? She will not leave until she knows Donnie is going to pull through.

At 9:15, Mrs. Daniels decides to take the boys home with her. They are hungry and tired but they did not want to leave their mom's side. "You boys go on home with grandma and as soon as your dad comes out of surgery I will call you, okay."

After six hours of surgery, the doctor makes his way out to the waiting area to give the family the news. "The bullet entered Donnie's lower abdomen and has damaged one of his kidneys and part of his liver. Donnie has been admitted to the Intense Care Unit where he will be monitored every hour on the hour. Your husband has been heavily sedated, but once he comes too, you will need to talk to him about a kidney transplant. We can put him on the list as soon as you let us know, but I would not wait too long to make a decision. As far as his liver I tried as best as I could to repair it but there are not guarantees that what I did will do the job."

The doctor walks away, allowing Danielle to go back to see her husband.

When she enters the room and walks closer to his bed, she feels her heart stop. Donnie looks pale. He has lost so much blood that he had to have a blood transfusion. Danielle walks over and touches his face. She leans down to kiss him gently on the lips as a tear drops on his cheek. "I'm sorry sweetheart. This is my fault. I will never forgive myself for the trouble I have caused this family."

Danielle goes back to the waiting room, "You guys can go on home I'm going to spend the night here. I will call you tomorrow when he awakes."

Danielle tries to make herself comfortable in the chair as she sits there watching her husband. She dozes off a couple of times but the nurses coming in and out of Donnie's room awake her.

Around 6 a.m., Danielle hears the faint sound of someone calling her name. She opens her eyes to find her husband looking at her.

Danielle hops out of the chair and runs to his side. "Good morning sweetheart." "How are you feeling?"

"I'm in pain," he says.

Danielle calls for the nurse to come in, "My husband is in a lot of pain. Is there anything you can give him?"

"Let me check with his doctor," the nurse says.

Later that afternoon, the family is back at the hospital to see Donnie. Only two people at a time are allowed back to his room. Jordan has just stepped outside of Donnie's room when Danielle enters.

Danielle moves over to his bed and out the corner of her eye, she sees a shadow move. She turns to look just in time to see Brenda rush out of Donnie's room dressed in a nurse's uniform.

"You fucking bitch," Danielle yells loud enough for Jordan who is walking down the hall to hear.

Danielle rushes out after Brenda as she tries to escape down the hall when she collides with a hard muscular body.

"Jordan stop her." "Don't let her get away!" Jordan grabs a hold of Brenda while Mark calls the police.

"You are one stupid bitch," Danielle says as she slaps the living daylights out of Brenda. "I can't believe you have the audacity to show your face after all the trouble you have caused."

Mark holds Danielle back fearing she will put a hurt on Brenda.

CHAPTER 31

"Hey Candy, this is Jasmine, I'm calling because I need a huge favor. I need a knock - out dress for a Christmas party that I am attending on Friday, but I have not been able to find the perfect dress. I need you help desperately. Call me on my cell when you get this message, Bye."

Wednesday evening when Jasmine arrives home, there was a fed ex package on the doorstep. She grabs the package under her arm and unlocks the front door. She makes her way to the family room dumping her belongings onto the sofa.

She opens the package to find the perfect Donna Karan red superfine Jersey floor length dress with a pair of Jimmy Choo Trina Pointy toe Jewel shoes. She is speechless. She knows she can count on her cousin to outdo herself.

Jasmine rushes up stair to try on the dress. She walks over to the full-length mirror and cannot believe how the dress looks on her. "Perfect," she says.

Later that evening, Jasmines receives a call from her cousin Candy. "So what do you think?"

"Candy, oh my God." "How is it that you can always pick the perfect outfit for me?"

"Like I always say, I know you better than you know yourself."

Both women laugh.

"How much did this cost me?"

"Let's just say it is an early wedding gift.

Jasmine rolls her eyes, "Do you know something that I don't?"

"No, I just have a feeling that your life is about to take a turn for the best."

"Okay, now you're sounding just like your aunt." "I think it is about time you come down for one of your weekend visits. There is so much that I have to fill you in on. You can stay at my place so that you can have your privacy."

"What's going on? I can tell by the sound of your voice that something is bothering you."

"Well, I haven't seen my period but it's only a few days late, I have been getting sick a lot lately."

"Oh my God," Candy screams. We're having a baby."

"Don't get ahead of yourself Candy. It is a little too early to say that. I will give it a couple of days and if she hasn't showed up then I will take a home pregnancy test."

"Well if you find out that you are, how will you feel about that?"

"I'm not sure right now. There's so much that's going on between Jordan and me. I just don't know how I would feel. This week has been perfect, but just the week before, his ex-confronted me at work. She had the nerve to show up here and tell me that she still has Jordan's heart and that he will never be able to commit himself to anyone as long as she has his heart. She also is claiming to be carrying his child, but Jordan has not said a word to me about the baby. To be honest, I'm not sure he is over her as much as he tries to make me believe his is."

"Oh I see, I guess I should make a trip down there and beat some sense into Jordan. Let me check my calendar and I will get back with you."

"All right and thanks again for everything." "I love you."

"I love you too little cuz, you hang in there okay."

"I will talk with you later, bye."

After Jasmine ends the call with Candy, she receives a call from Roberto. "Hey Roberto, what's going on?"

"Jas, I'm not trying to start any rumors or cause any problems but I think you should know that Jordan and Vanessa are at the Cheesecake Factory having dinner together. If it were anyone else I wouldn't care but I don't want to see you get hurt."

He knows he has hit a nerve when Jasmines tone changes from friendly to cold. "You know what Roberto, Jordan is a grown man and he can have dinner with whomever he chooses."

"I know, but I just wanted you to be aware of it."

"Thanks Roberto for telling me this," she says sarcastically and hangs up the phone.

Jasmine phones Jordan several times and it goes straight to voicemail. "Oh, too busy to answer your phone I see."

Jordan arrives home a little after nine. He comes through the door to find Jasmine standing there with her arms folded across her chest. "I'm sorry sweetheart that I missed your calls but I was in a meeting."

"A meeting, just stop it right now Jordan, you are not a good liar. What were you and Vanessa meeting about at the Cheesecake Factory?"

Jordan is speechless. He cannot tell Jasmine the truth about him having dinner with Vanessa but it is an innocent dinner date.

"What, so now you're spying on me. You know what I am a grown ass man and if I choose to have dinner with someone that is my choice."

~ cclxxx ~

"Yeah, you are right. You can have dinner with whomever you chose and so can I," Jasmine says as she storms upstairs to their bedroom.

The next morning Jordan awakes early, he notice Jasmines side of the bed has not been touched. He makes his way down the hall to the guest room to find her but there is no Jasmine. He goes downstairs to the family room where he finds Jasmine asleep on the sofa. Jordan pulls the cover over Jasmine careful not to wake her. He stands there admiring the woman he plans to make his wife. He feels bad about what he had said to her last night, but how can he tell her that he had met with Vanessa for dinner to tell her that he will no longer stand by and watch her torment Jasmine and that he has plans to marry her. He wanted to make it loud and clear to Vanessa that there is no chance they would get back together and that she needed to move on with her life because he had.

After his dinner, Jordan made a stop at Tiffany's, where he purchased a diamond Marquise engagement ring to present to her at his company's Christmas party.

Jasmine awakes to the smell of brewing coffee. She hears Jordan fumbling around in the kitchen and decides to avoid him and make her way upstairs where she showered, dressed and was out the door before Jordan had a chance to speak with her.

Jasmine pulls into the parking lot of CVS where she spots a black Lexis that she has seen parked down the street from Jordan's pulling in beside her and wonders if she is being followed. She quickly dismisses the thought when she notices a woman with a child get out of the car. Jasmine goes inside the store and finds the aisle where the pregnancy tests are. She hesitates a minute before grabbing the kit and heads to the checkout counter.

Back in her car, Jasmine pulls out the kit and begins reading the instructions, while trying to kill time until she thinks Jordan has left for work.

Jasmine phones Patricia and leaves a message that she will not be in today and heads home. She wants to have all of her belongings move back into her apartment before Jordan returns home this evening.

Jasmine spent most of the morning moving her things back into her apartment. By noon, she has finished and has completely forgotten about checking the results of the pregnancy test that she has left back at Jordan's. She grabs her keys and heads over to Jordan's.

Jasmine walks upstairs to the bathroom and takes a seat on the side of the bathtub as she prepares herself for the result.

She grabs the box and read the instruction again blue negative pink positive. As she examines the stick she feels as if her heart is about to stop. Jasmine is carrying Jordan's child. "Oh my God," she says repeatedly. Jasmine continues to sit on the edge of the bathtub in disbelief until pangs of hunger hit her.

~ cclxxxii ~

Jasmine is in the kitchen preparing her some lunch when the doorbell rings. "Who can this be?" she says aloud. She makes her way to the front door, when she opens the door; she finds a man standing there dressed in black with a ski mask covering his face.

Fear settles in as she tries to shut the door but the man's strength over powers her. The mask man kicks the door open and swings at Jasmine missing her. Jasmines throws a hard punch to his face hitting him right above his eye. Jasmine turns to runs toward the kitchen but the blow to the back of her head knocks her to the floor where the assailant continues to beat her until she is unconscious.

The mask man ties Jasmine up and drags her body to the front door. Her assailant steps out onto the porch to check out his surroundings to make sure there is no one in sight before putting her body into the back of his trunk.

CHAPTER 32

Jasmine wakes three hours later in an unfamiliar place tied to a bed. Her face and body in pain from the blows that she suffered. Jasmine glances around the room. It is cold and gloomy and the only sight of light comes from upstairs under a closed door. She thinks this has all been a bad dream until she tries to move from the bed. She wonders who would do something like to this to her. She has never hurt anyone. Then her mind thinks about Vanessa. This is her way of getting me out of Jordan's life altogether. She begins to cry and when she thinks about her unborn child, her crying becomes louder. It is as if she is reliving her life over again with her ex, that time she ended up in the hospital not in someone's basement.

Jordan phoned Jasmine several times that afternoon before heading home to check on her. As he enters his home, everything is silent. He calls out to Jasmine a few times before heading upstairs. He checks their bedroom and finds all of her belongings are gone. He then checks the guest room and it is empty as well. However, what he did find stuns him. He finds the pregnancy test that lay on the bathroom sink. Jordan picks the stick up and notices that it is pink he knows enough to know that this means positive. He rushes back downstairs to the kitchen when he notices the blood that has splatter against the wall. After searching the house inside and out, Jordan has a bad feeling that something is terribly wrong. He puts a call in to his brother and Ronnie.

Later that evening after calling the hospitals and Danielle and Jasmines parents, there is still no word on her whereabouts.

"How far can she have gone without her car and who flatten all of her tires?" Ronnie asks.

"This doesn't sit well with me," Matthew says. "Where did this blood come from?"

"I don't know and to make matters worse, Jasmine is pregnant, I found the pregnancy test upstairs in the guest bathroom."

"Do you have a set of keys to her apartment?" Ronnie asks.

"Yes, I have them upstairs."

"I think we need to take a ride over there."

When the men enter Jasmines apartment, they know in their guts that something bad has taken place. Jasmines furniture and her clothes have been ripped to shreds. The writing on the wall tells it all. In bright red letters read: Jordan I have taken your precious girl and you will never see her again. Jordan drops to his knees and grabs his chest. "Who would do this to her?" He asks repeatedly.

~ cclxxxvi ~

"Jordan you have to stay calm and think. Can you think of enemies she may have?"

"No, everyone loves her you know that." Ronnie stands there in disbelief while Matthew places a call to the chief of police.

In no time, Jasmines apartment is surrounding by police officers and detectives. They interrogated Jordan as if he is their number one suspect. "I'm sorry bro, but you know as well as I do that they have to treat you as a suspect until you are cleared of any wrong doings." Matthew says as he stands over Jordan.

After thirty minutes of interrogating Jordan, several detectives follow him back to his home where he shows them the blood splatter on the wall.

After the detective confirms Jordan's whereabouts with his secretary, his is off the hook for now. The chief of police, who has known Jordan since he was a young boy, apologizes. "You know son, my men were just doing their job. There is no doubt in my mind that you are innocent."

"What are your men going to do now chief?"

"We are going to do everything possible to find Ms. Smith and if there is anything you can think of that will help, please do not hesitate to call me."

"I almost forgot about this, but she had a break in a few weeks ago. We filed a police report but nothing ever became of it."

"Yeah, I am aware of that. You know Jasmine's dad and I go way back so he has already filled me in on this. I am heading over to see him now. I think it would be best if I broke the news to her parents."

"You know that's the reason she moved in with me so she would be safe but I screwed up. I didn't protect her. I didn't keep her safe."

"Don't you go blaming yourself. You had no way of knowing that this would happen. None of us did? If her dad didn't feel that you could protect her, he would have moved her in with them. You have to keep your head up and think positive and in no time, she will be back with you before you know it. You know your brother will be on the case and he will not rest until he finds her." The chief of police pats Jordan on the shoulder as he heads out to talk with Jasmine's parents.

Jasmines cries are heard upstairs. The mask man opens the basement door and walks down. "You can cry as loud as you want my dear. No one will hear you."

"Why have you done this to me? What have I ever done to you?" The mask man walks over to Jasmines and takes a seat on the side of the bed.

"My sweet Jasmine. You are so naïve. You and Jordan have caused me and my family so much pain over the years and today, is your day to pay for it. However, Jordan has been paying for this for the last couple of months and he didn't even know it. Eventually he caught on and hired that private detective that he has everyone believing is his auditor."

~ cclxxxviii ~

"What did we do to cause you and your family so much pain?"

Just then, Jasmine recognizes her assailant's voice.

"Roberto is that you"?

He pulls off his mask, "No bitch it's Robert!"

Jasmines vision is still blurry from the swelling to both eyes but she definitely recognizes that it is Roberto or Robert as he calls himself.

"Roberto, why have you done this to me? I thought we were friends?"

"Jasmine we could never be friends. You and your lover boy were the cause of my father's death. I made a promise to myself that one day I would make Jordan and you pay for it."

"What are you talking about?"

"I guess you don't remember me from back in the day. You use to be a little tease back then walking around with those little tight shorts half way covering your ass. So one day I took you up on what you were offering. Jordan comes home early and accuses me of trying to rape you. Do you remember now?" Jordan ran and told my dad and three days later, he commits suicide. It was all because of what Jordan had told him. I waited for years to get my revenge, I changed my name to Roberto and got hired on at Jordan's company so that I could robbed him blind and watch as his company that he worked so hard for go down the drain, but when I saw you at the airport and later you showed up at work. I just knew something was going on between the two of you. That is when I decided to take you away from him. I figure this would be the sweetest revenge to be able to get both of you. What makes this even sweeter is that Jordan will never see his unborn child."

Jasmines mouth drops open. "How did you know that I was carrying Jordan's child?"

"I know everything; I know every move you two made. Scary isn't it?"

"Please Roberto don't do anything to harm me and my child. This child means everything to me. I have waited so long for this. Don't make us pay for something that we had no control over."

"Please don't beg. It doesn't become you."

Roberto eases up from the bed and makes his way to the steps. He turns back around to look at the woman who had gotten under his skin. He tries hard to fight the feeling that runs through him each time he thinks about what he has done to her. He turns around just in time as a tear falls from his eye. He begins to think about his dad and knows that his dad would be so disappointed in his behavior today, but what is done is done. He cannot go back and change things. If he let her go, he knows it will not be long before he would be behind bars.

~ CCXC ~

Later that evening, the family gathered over at Jordan's along with Jasmine's parents. Still no word on Jasmines whereabouts. Jordan grows tired sitting around doing nothing.

"You guys can stay her if you want, but I am not going to sit around and wait on the police to find Jasmine," Jordan says. He grabs his coat and heads out the door.

"Hey Jordan wait up, I will ride with you". Ronnie says.

As they ride around the streets of Indianapolis, Ronnie asks the dreadful question. "Is there a reason Jasmine was not at work today?" The look on Jordan's face tells Ronnie everything he needs to know.

"I thought she was until around nine this morning when Patricia tells me that she had called in. Last night she accused me of still wanting Vanessa because she found out that Vanessa and I had dinner yesterday evening."

"What!"

"It was innocent; I just wanted Vanessa to know that there was no way we would ever get back together and that I was planning to ask Jasmine to marry me. I wanted her to know so that she could stop all the nonsense with Jasmine because my mind is made up. After that I went and purchased a ring for Jasmine at Tiffany's." Ronnie's heart went out to Jordan.

"Well just hold on to it. You'll get the opportunity to ask her to be your wife."

Three hours later, Jordan pulls into his driveway. "Why don't you go inside and get some rest. We can start bright and early tomorrow morning."

"All right man," Jordan says as he makes his way out of the car. Ronnie feels for his friend. He knows how he would feel if this had happened to him. He also knows Jordan would be right by his side giving him support.

Later that night, Ronnie checks his messages and to his surprise, there is a message from Mr. Jones, the banking center manager asking Ronnie to come into the banking center tomorrow morning.

Earlier that afternoon, Roberto and Alexis had gone into the banking to cash a couple of checks drawn on Jordan's account but was stopped when the alert came across the system that there is fraudulent activity on this account and that every check has to be approved. Roberto and Alexis stand nervously waiting for the bank teller to return. When she finally returns the manager with her caused the two to panic and run out of the banking center leaving their ids behind.

By the time Roberto gets home, he has calmed down. The only evidence they had was that they know what the two look like. He was well aware that they had left their ids that contained false information thanks to his friend at the bureau of motor vehicle.

Roberto continues to take his frustration out on Jasmine by withholding food and water from her.

Jasmine continues to cry out for food and water. She is hungry and wet from urinating on herself.

"How can you treat me like I'm some dog out on the street? I have pissed all over myself. You don't even have the decency to allow me to go to the restroom. What kind of monster are you?"

Robert and Alexis sit at the kitchen table listening to Jasmine run off at the mouth. He chuckles, "She is a feisty one," he says to Alexis. Alexis did not want any part of the kidnapping. Writing bad checks was one thing but kidnapping was not up her alley.

"Robert, why don't you give her something to eat, drink and allow her to go to the restroom.   How would you feel if someone had done this to me?"

"I don't know why you are feeling so soft hearted when you know what has to happen to her."

"What do you mean?"

"If I were to let her go, how fast do you think it would be before we were behind bars?"

"So what are you planning to do?" Robert looks at her with a devilish look.

"No, Robert, this was not the plan."

"First of all, you need to stop calling me Robert. You know I have changed my name to Roberto.   What do you suggest we do, Miss know it all?"

Alexis sits there thinking. She has to come up with something because there is no way she is going down for murder.

Denise Hill

CHAPTER 33

Jordan sits alone by the fireplace as the tears begin to fall from his eyes. He has already consumed four beers and is on his fifth one when his phone rang. He lets the phone ring and ring off the hook. He is in no mood to speak with anyone unless they have news on Jasmines whereabouts. "How could I have been so stupid?" "If I had not had dinner with Vanessa, Jasmine would have not been upset and would have shown up to work and none of this would have happened," he says aloud as she throws a beer can at the wall. Jordan sits there and thinks about the good times they shared together and how Jasmine has changed him for the better.

Jordan continues to sit most of the night going over in his head where and who could have done this. Can this be connected to the embezzlement? He thinks. Jordan grabs his phone to call Matthew but realize it is two in the morning.

Jordan gets up from the floor and makes his way over to the couch where stretches out and continues to wreck his brain as he falls into a deep sleep.

The next morning before Roberto leaves for work. He prepares Jasmine some breakfast and change the soil bed covers. He even allows her to roam the basement freely.

Jasmine inhales her food and milk but within an hour, she feels sick to her stomach. Her body is weak, her eyes are still swollen and her ribs feel inflamed, but she is thankful that Roberto allows her to move around the room. Now she has to find a way to get out before he makes it home from work. The thought of her never seeing Jordan and her unborn child gives her the strength she needs to survive. She continues to pray to God for strength and ask for the will power to overcome what has been done to her.

Jasmine begins to examine the room. There are no windows to escape out of so that idea is out. There has to be something that she is overlooking. She thinks.

As she sits back down on the bed, she hears a noise coming from the corner of the room. It startles her. Then she thinks she is losing her mind, but she hears the sound again. Jasmine moves closer to where the noise is coming from. As she gets closer, she can tell that it is a woman's cry for help. The cry is coming from behind the bookshelf, but how can that be she questions herself.

Jasmine begins to look at the bookshelf closer. With the little strength that she has, she tries to move the bookshelf out of the way, but in doing so causes the secret door to slightly open. Jasmine peeps inside but her vision is not the best because of the swelling all she can see is pure darkness. "Hey I hear you in there but I can't see anything."

Jasmine stands there until she hears the cry again. It is a woman's cry. The woman's cries become louder as Jasmine goes further into the room. The room smells horrible. She is waiting for some creature to jump out at her at any time. Jasmine continues to walk in darkness "Hey where are you?" Jasmine yells out. Out of nowhere, Jasmine feels a touch on her leg that scares the shit out of her. Jasmine grabs her chest before kneeling down to feel a pair of hands tied together.

"You will have to keep it down in here before he comes back and hears you. I will do everything I can to get you out of there, just hold on". Jasmine works with the rope to untie her hands she unties her feet and help the woman to stand. She walks her out of the room and is surprise to see another woman that has been badly beaten.

"Oh my God!" "How long have you been in there?"

From the smell of the room, Jasmine can tell that she must have been there for at least two to three weeks. The woman shakes her head. "What is your name?"

Jasmine asks the woman as she escorts her to the bathroom where she helps her into the shower. "Toni, my name is Toni," the woman says. I am so hungry; I haven't eaten since I have been here."

"Well, I don't have any food to give you but I do have some milk that you can have. Jasmine gives her the left over milk that she could not get down. I do not have any extra clothes either. We have got to find a way out of here," Jasmine tells her. Just then, Jasmine hears the sound of a car door shutting.

"Oh, you have to get back in there before he sees that you are out." Jasmines guides Toni back to the hidden room and close the door. However, Toni's cries are so loud that Jasmine is afraid that Roberto will find out that she knows about her.

"Please be quiet. He can't know that I know about you. He will surely kill us both. I will come for you when the coast is clear."

Jasmine walks back over to the bed just as Roberto opens the basement door.

"What are you up to down there?" Roberto yells from the top of the stairs.

Jasmine did not even attempt to say anything. Roberto leaves the basement door open as he prepares lunch for her.

"I know you must be hungry, so I am making you some lunch before I head back to work. I thought you should know that Jordan didn't show up for work today. Imagine that," Roberto says sarcastically.

As Roberto climbs down the stairs with her lunch, Jasmine wonders why he is being so thoughtful. Maybe he is trying to poison me she thinks.

Roberto lays the food on the table beside her bed. "Eat up," he says. "I will be back later around dinner time." Jasmine rolls her eyes at him. The look of disgust is written all over her face. "Now don't be like that Jasmine, I did what I had to do. I'm sorry that it had to turn out like this because I was beginning to like you."

After Jasmine hears Roberto pull off, she quickly pushes the secret door open. She walks Toni back to the bed.

"Here, he made this lunch for me I'll share it with you. It's not much but it is better than nothing. In the meantime, we have got to find a way out of here."

Jasmine leaves Toni on the bed as she makes her way into the secret room.

"Toni, we have got to find a way out of here tonight if we are going to survive."

Toni sits on the bed. Deep down inside, Toni has already lost the will to survive.

Jasmine on the other hand has will enough for the both of them to survive. The thought of her not seeing her unborn child and Jordan is enough will for her to survive.

She walks further into the room in search of a way out.

The room is dark and cold. She cannot believe someone can be so cruel to keep a human being in a place like this, but she now knows that she is dealing with cold-blooded person. As she moves further into the room she bumps into several boxes causing them to tumble down up on her, but in doing so, sunlight peaks through a boarded window that had been covered by the boxes.

"Oh my God, I have found a way out for us," Jasmine shouts.

The only obstacle is being able to reach the window. Jasmine stacks the boxes on top of each other and climbs on top to end up falling through the empty boxes.

"I need something sturdy," she thinks a loud.

~ CCC ~

Jasmine searches frantically, but not being able to see is hindering her search. Jasmine goes further into the room feeling for anything that she can stand on top of to reach the window. As she continues searching, she comes across some crates.

"This should do the job; I just hope I can fit through the small window."

Jasmine stacks three crates on top of each other under the window. The crates are much higher than the boxes so it is hard for her to climb on top. She removes one crate making it easier for her to stand on it. She struggles to remove the boards from the window, but with her determination, she is able to remove the three boards.

Jasmine has spent so much time searching the room that she forgets about Roberto until she hears the sound of a car door slamming.

Jasmine jumps down without any thought to her injuries, she yells in agony as she grabs her side and makes her way back to Toni.

"I think he's coming, I have to put you back in the room, but don't worry, tonight I will get us help."

Later that night when everything is quiet, Jasmine enters the secret room to make her escape.

"Toni, I am going through this window and when I return, I will have help for you. Whatever you do, please keep quiet."

Jasmine breaks the window with one of the boards and crawls out. As she stands, she feels weak and lightheaded but she knows this is not the time to give in to her symptoms. Jasmine heads for the woods that surround the house. She has no clue as to where she is but she knows if she continues to move she will eventually find help.

Roberto awakes to the sound of glass breaking, he jumps out bed and slips his slippers on and heads downstairs.

He listens as he searches each room when he hears Toni's voice.

"How the hell did she get out of the room," he thinks as he opens the basement door. Standing at the bottom step, he sees the secret door open and Toni sitting there crying.

Roberto grabs the flashlight from the drawer and heads inside where he sees the window broken. He knows Jasmine has escaped but he doesn't know how far she has gotten.

Robert rushes back upstairs, grabs his coat and heads for the back. He knows these woods like the back of his hand. He use to come and hide out in the woods after receiving one of his dads beating which was almost everyday.

Jasmine has to stop for air. She is exhausted, cold and in pain and she has no idea where she is but she knows she has to move on. She continues moving when she sees headlights. Jasmine is ecstatic. She knows if she can reach the street, she can flag down a car for help. Jasmine picks up speed and as she gets closer to the street, everything goes black.

Roberto was deep in the woods; he was giving up hope of finding Jasmine when fear set in about going to prison. He began to remember what his dad had taught him about tracking predicators in the woods. "Listen son listen," his dad would constantly tell him. Listen to the sound of the leaving and the breaking of the tree branches. This will tell you which direction your prey is headed. Once Roberto remembered this, it wasn't hard for Roberto to find out where Jasmine was. He heard the sound of the leaves and the breaking of the tree branches. Jasmine was almost to the street when Roberto approached her from behind and slammed a

thick tree branched against the back of her head knocking her out cold.

When Jasmine awakes, she is right where she started, in the basement tied to the bed.

Jasmine opens her eyes to find Roberto standing over her.

"Nice try Jasmine. I let you roam the basement freely, but you have been a bad girl so I have no choice but to keep you tied to this bed," Roberto says as he makes his way upstairs.

CHAPTER 34

Ronnie sits in the parking lot of the banking center waiting for it to open. He decides to phone Jordan to see how he is doing. When Jordan does not answer, he calls him at work and is told that Jordan has not made it in. Ronnie pulls out of the parking lot and heads out to Jordan's. He has not been able to contact Jordan since he left him last night and he is worried.

Ronnie knocks at Jordan's door several times but there is no answer. He knows he is in there but he does not know what condition he is in. Ronnie looks around the porch under the flower pot looking for a spare key. He remembers Jordan telling him that he keeps a spare key there, but that spare key is gone. This makes him worry even more. He reaches for his phone and dials Jordan's number again. Surprisingly Jordan answers.

"Hey man, open up, I'm at the front door."

Jordan staggers to the door. Before Ronnie can get in good, he can smell the liquor seeping through Jordan's pores. "Man you smell of liquor." "Are those the same clothes you had on yesterday?" Jordan ignores Ronnie and walks into the family room where he has been since he left Ronnie yesterday. Ronnie follows him into the family room where he has to scoot beer cans and a liquor bottle out of the way in order to take a seat on the couch. "I know you are feeling down right now, but this is not the answer," Ronnie says as he holds up the liquor bottle. I need you to get yourself together and take a ride with me to have a talk with Mr. Jones. He left me a message yesterday evening that he wants to meet with me first thing this morning. He may be on to something."

"Alright let me run up and change."

"Make sure you shower!"

Ronnie and Jordan enter the banking center where Mr. Jones greets them. "I am so glad you made it. I have the suspects on camera along with the check they tried to cash yesterday."

The two follow Mr. Jones to his office. Jordan is stunned when he recognizes one of the suspects. "That's Alexis but I am not sure who the guy is," Jordan says."

"Who is Alexis," Ronnie asks. "She is the housekeeper that I hired and fired a few days ago for breaking into my office."

"Do you have her address?"

"Yeah, I have it on file at the office."

"Well I suggest we take a ride to see her."

"Thanks Mr. Jones, we will be in touch," Jordan says shaking Mr. Jones' hand.

Jordan and Ronnie are in his office as Roberto passes by. He is shock to see Jordan in the office today. Roberto stands outside of Jordan's office to listen.

Jordan pulls up the file with Alexis's information, "Alexis Johnson, here we go. She lives at 5642 N. Emerson Ave."

"I say we make a surprise visit to Ms. Johnson."

"I can't believe she is in on this. She is such a nice girl."

"Well, the nice and quiet ones are the ones you need to watch out for," Ronnie comments.

Roberto runs to his cubicle and phones Alexis on her cell phone. "Hey sis, Jordan and Ronnie are on the way to the house. They know you are involved in the embezzlement."

"Oh shit!" "What I am going to do?" Jordan knows that I work at the hospital part time. Hell I can't afford to have him and the police show up here after me."

"Just stay calm I will think of something and call you right back."

Robert calls Alexis back within five minutes.

"Hey sis, I'm afraid that when Jordan goes to the house and you are not there the hospital will be there next stop so you are going to have to leave. See if you can take a few days off until things die down. You cannot go back to the house so get a hotel preferably close to the airport and check back with me once you have done that. I will stick around here to see if I learn more about their search for you. Call me back once you have settled in."

"But what are we going to do about our guest at the house?"

"Don't worry I will take care of that since no one suspects me."

"Okay, I will call you when I am settled."

Roberto sits back in his chair. This has not turned out the way he had planned. He continues to wonder how they know Alexis is in on this.

When Jordan and Ronnie arrive at the address, Jordan remembers coming here when he was much younger but he cannot remember why.

"Man this house seems so familiar to me but I don't know why."

They knock at the door several times and get no answer. "I know Alexis works at the hospital, so let's try our luck there."

Alexis pulls out of the hospital-parking garage just as Jordan's car turns the corner heading in her direction. "Oh my God", Alexis turns her car in the opposite direction and speeds away. By this time her heart is beating fast her palms are sweaty, she is a nervous wreck and begins to panic. "I cannot go to jail, I 'm not cut out for this shit. Why did I let my brother talk me into this shit anyway? If he wanted revenge, he should have done this by his damn self." She continues to drive and talk to herself aloud while she repeatedly looks in her rearview mirror to make sure she is not being followed.

It was Christmas Eve; two weeks had gone by still no word on Jasmine's whereabouts. Ronnie and Matthew had made several visits to the home where Alexis lived but was unable to catch her. They find out that she has quit her job at the hospital. Jordan remembers Alexis telling him that she has a brother so Ronnie and Matthew had questioned several of the neighbors and find out that her brother is Roberto Johnson, one of Jordan's employees.

The next morning Jordan, Ronnie, and, Matthew sit in Jordan's office waiting on Roberto's arrival. Little did they know, Roberto has been parked down the street watching their every move and knows things are getting ready to blow up in his face so going back to work was not an option.

Jordan is at his moms trying to enjoy himself but it is hard knowing that the woman he loves and his unborn child are missing or even worse dead.

Matthew and Ronnie have worked hard trying to find Jasmine but each time they came up short.

Jasmine's parents are worried sick. Her mom has suffered a heart attack and is not doing well. This Christmas will be like no other for the Daniels and Smith family.

Jasmine is trying to hold on to what little life she has left. Toni is almost gone Jasmine knows she had to do something quick or it would be over for the both of them.

The house is quiet, each day Roberto spent less and less time there, which would be perfect if she was not tied to the bed.

Alexis has been cooped up in the motel for days. Roberto tells her that she needs to lay low for awhile until things died down a little, but she needs to get out and clear her head. She has been unable to sleep or eat knowing that two women in their home would eventually die. She did not want this on her conscience.

While Roberto is asleep, she grabs the keys and head out.

As Alexis turns the corner to her street, she surveys the area closely making sure there are no cops in sight. She pulls into the driveway and sits for a minute before getting out. Ronnie and Matthew sit outside Alexis's home when they notice a car pulling in the driveway. They see a figure of a petite woman exiting the car and running to the back of the house.

"Man that's probably Alexis." Matthews says as he and Ronnie jump out of the car.

Jasmine awakes when she hears the sound of glass breaking. She is afraid she hears footsteps running upstairs and then realizes someone has broken in. Should I call out for help or would it better to keep quiet she asks herself. She continues to question herself when she hears the sound of the door unlock. She closes her eyes as she listens to footsteps creep down the steps. They stop but she is too afraid to open her eyes, but when her hands are cut lose, she opens her eyes to find a young girl who looks alike like Alexis at her side and without a word she tells Jasmine to run upstairs.

"Ronnie you stay here while I go around back."

Matthew makes his way to the back where it is pitch black. Without his flashlight, he is unable to see anything. Matthew returns to the front with Ronnie. "Man, I say we kick this motherfucker in."

"You took the words right out of my mouth," Ronnie replies.

Just then, Jasmine hears a loud noise. She hears two male voices and the sound of a car speeding off.

Open the door a voice within her says. Jasmine is weak and ready to keel over at any moment. She climbs up the steps and stops at the top. She reaches her hand up to the doorknob and turns it. To her surprise, it opens. "Oh my God," she says. Jasmine calls out to Toni who is locked away in the secret room.

Matthew takes off after Alexis while Ronnie is still in the house. He walks around when he hears a faint voice of a female. "Who's there?" Ronnie asks.

"Help us please." "We are down here."   Ronnie walks toward the sound of the woman voice. He feels along the wall to keep himself from stumbling. As he gets closer, he finds a light switch on the wall. When the lights come on his heart drops to his stomach.

It's Jasmine she looks like "death eating crackers."

"Jasmine is that you?"

"Ronnie, oh my God help us."

Ronnie grabs Jasmine up in his arms and heads back to the living room. "No, don't leave her." Ronnie is confused.

"Don't leave who?"

"Toni, she's downstairs in the secret room." Ronnie sits Jasmine down and grabs his phone. He calls the police and the paramedics.

"Where's Jordan?" Jasmine asks.

"Oh shit, I almost forgot." Ronnie phones Jordan at his mom's.

Denise Hill

CHAPTER 35

"Where have you been, I have been worried sick about you?"

"I was out riding around, just thinking."

"What is this," Robert asks as he pulls his sister's jacket off. "You are bleeding. You have been to the house haven't you, but how did you get in since I took your keys?" Alexis walks into the bathroom to wipe the blood from her arm.

"I haven't been to the house I had this jacket in my trunk." Roberto grabs his jacket and heads out.

"Where are you going?"

Roberto knows his sister too well. He also knows she has been acting weird lately. He just hopes she hasn't done what he thinks she has done.

Jordan's cell rings four times before he answers. "Jordan, this is Ronnie, I have found Jasmine. She is alive."

"You found Jasmine!" Jordan says loudly.

Everyone in the room is silent as they run to where Jordan stands. "Where is she?"

"She's at Alexis and Roberto's. Roberto kidnapped her and the woman from the banking center, Toni Reynolds."

Roberto sits parked down the street from his house. Police cars surround the street. He knows his sister has allowed the women to escape but what he cannot understand is why.

Roberto makes his way back to the motel to find his sister in tears. "Alexis how can you do this to us?"

"Roberto this is your plan not mine. I don't want to go to jail for murder. I agreed to help you cash those checks but that was it. You were going to kill them and I couldn't sit back and let you do that."

"Well, by now the police are probably out looking for the both of us. You know we have to go to plan B."

"Plan B what is plan B?"

"We will have to leave the country or face going to prison for a long time."

"Leave the country." "Are you out of your mind?"

"Don't worry I have everything already taken care of just in case things didn't go as planned. Our flight leaves in two hours so get you together so we can head out."

"Where are we going?"

"Jamaica, I have some friends that will take good care of us until we get on our feet." Alexis did not want to leave the United States. She did not want to leave her family or friends.

The Daniels and the Smith family have arrived at the hospital fifteen minutes after Jasmine and Toni had arrived.

Jordan paces back and forth in the waiting room waiting to hear word on Jasmine's condition. He is fearful of his unborn child's life after speaking with Ronnie about the condition he had found Jasmine in. He knows having kids means the world to her. He can only hope and pray that the both of them are okay.

Hours go by and still no word from the doctor. "Excuse me miss, but can you tell me when I will be able to see Jasmine Smith?"

"Sir, the doctor will be out in a few minutes to speak with the family."

"Is she going to be okay?"

"Sir, the doctor will talk with you about her condition."

Jordan is speaking to his brother Matthew. He tells Jordan that the police have captured Alexis and Roberto at Motel 8.

"They were on their way out of the country. Can you believe that? That is not the best part, Roberto Johnson aka Robert Johnson."

"Robert Johnson," Jordan says.

"Yeah, remember he tried to rape Jasmine years ago and you told his dad and later he committed suicide. Well he blamed you for that. This is why he tried to destroy you. He wanted to rob you blind but when Jasmine came back to town and he found out the two of you were a couple. This made his revenge even sweeter."

Jordan continued to pace back and forth trying to digest what he has learned about Roberto and Alexis until the doctor made his way out to speak with the family.

"Hi, I am Dr. Thompson and I will be Ms. Smith physician while she is here with us."

"Jasmine has suffered severe fractures to her ribs. I have confirmed that she is three weeks into her pregnancy but since there is a significant amount of arsenic in her system, the survival rate for the baby is unlikely." By chance, she does carry the baby full term there is a 50% chance that the baby will suffer from retardation. I have made Jasmine aware of the situation and I am awaiting her decision on whether she will abort the baby or if she will try to carry the baby to term."

Jordan puts his hands up to his face. He is saddened by the news, but he is grateful that Jasmine is found alive.

As Jordan enters the room, his heart aches for Jasmine because he knows how much she wants a baby.

"Hey sweetheart." "How are you feeling?"

"I have felt better," Jasmine says as she grabs a hold of Jordan's hand and smiles.

"I assume the doctor has spoken to you about the baby?"

"Yes, he has and I want you to know that whatever decision you make, I will support you 100%. Jasmine I need to know something. Why did you move your belongings back to your apartment?"

Tears begin to roll down her face. "When you told me that I made you whole, it was hard for me to believe that. I know you were only saying what you thought I wanted to hear and when I ran into Vanessa, she told me that she would always have your heart and that she was carrying your child. Then I learned that the two of you were out having dinner, I knew I could not compete with that."

Jordan wipes the tears from her eyes. "Listen Jasmine, Vanessa is not pregnant and if she is it is not mine. Trust me. The reason that I invited Vanessa to dinner was to let her know what my intention were with you. I told her that I would not stand by anymore and let her harass you. The few weeks that you were missing made me realize that it is you that I need and want in my life forever."

Jordan pulls the tiffany box out of his coat pocket.

"Jasmine you mean the world to me and always have. I know now not to take anything or anyone for granted, so with that being said, Ms. Smith will you marry me and make me the happiest man alive?"

"Jordan, do you know how long I have waited to hear you say those words? However, right now, we have a bigger issue to deal with. What if I cannot give you any kids. Would you still want to spend the rest of your life with me?"

"Children or no children, I know I want you in my life forever and if it comes to it we could always adopt."

"Now don't make me get down on my hands and knees and beg you, because I will."

Six months later

June 25, 2009

It was the end of June; the weather was perfect for an outdoor ceremony. The sunny is shining and the wind blows a cool breeze off the lake.

"Jasmine hold your gut in," Candy yells.

"I can't, I'm pregnant or haven't you noticed."

"Here, let me get it," Danielle says. Honey I hope this zipper doesn't pop."

"You guys sure know how to make a woman feel special on the most important day of her life," Jasmine says.

"I'm sorry cuz; I know you have been waiting for this day for a long time."

"You got that right and I will not let anything spoil this day for me, even if it means walking down the aisle naked."

"Oh my God, that would be an awful sight," Candy says jokingly.

Vanessa sat parked down the street from Jordan. She learns from Thomas that today is Jordan's and Jasmines wedding day. She is not invited, and has been warned to stay away. She feels so alone after giving birth to a daughter that she tried to pass off on Jordan as being the father but he knows better. After the baby was born, it was clear that the father was a white blue eyed man.

Thomas has quit his job at JD Processing and moved in with Vanessa but after the birth of their daughter, things started to go downhill for the couple. Thomas's family disowned the baby and urged Thomas to leave Vanessa. They say she is bad for his image. Vanessa's plan backfired on her and now she is left to care for her child alone the only support she has is her family.

Jasmine makes her way to the entrance behind the curtains. She stands there as Mark's soulful voice began to sing one of Jordan's favorite Brian McKnight songs, "Never Felt This Way."

~ CCCXX ~

Jasmine stands there looking in awe at all the people that have gathered for this special occasion. The Daniels sisters have out done themselves. The backyard has been turned into something so elegant.

Jasmine makes her way down the aisle to stand before the minister and next to her soon to be husband, who by the way, looks gorgeous.

The two exchanged their vows with one another and after the minister pronounce them husband and wife. The crowd stands and cheers. They know this has been a long time coming.

Epilogue

"Come on Jasmine push, you can do it."

Between breaths, Jasmine shouts, "Stop telling me what I can do!"

One hard push and the two welcomed into the world Jordan Denise Daniels.

"Oh my God, she is beautiful. She looks just like her dad," Jordan says.

Jordan is so proud. He doesn't know what to do with himself. No one could have told him that in the end, he would end up with the love of his life and a precious baby girl.

Jordan leaves the maternity room and finds a quiet place to be alone. He finds his way to a bathroom stall. In tears, he kneels down and gives God the praise for the deliverance of Jasmine and the birth of his baby girl.

"Father in the name of Jesus, I want to thank you for all that you have done. I know that without you, I would have lost them both. I can never repay you for the joy that you brought to my life. I will always try to live my life to please you and to help others as you have always helped my loved ones and me. I thank you father in the name of Jesus for your unconditional love and for all our blessings. I only wish my dad could be here to enjoy the birth of his granddaughter but I know he is looking down from heaven with a huge smile on his face. I ask you father in the name of Jesus to help me be the best father that I can be and help me be the best husband a man can be to his wife. I ask that you continue to guide me in the right direction and prepare my steps for me. I ask all these things in your sweet wonderful name. Amen."

New Year's Eve

Jordan gets out of his car and treads up the walkway. He is excited about surprising his wife with his first romance novel. He wants her to know that she is his inspiration for this book. As Jordan opens the door, he is welcomed with open arms by his wife.

"Hey handsome." "I'm glad you finally made it home," Jasmine says as she kisses her husband on the lips.

"I can get use to this, if you do this more often, I promise I will be home early every day."

"Alright you two, we still have work to do before your guest start arriving," Mrs. Smith says.

Jordan whispers into Jasmines ear, "You better be glad your mom came in here and saved you from me."

"Don't worry we can continue this tonight after our guest leave. So be ready."

"Be ready, I am already counting down the hours."

The two beam with pleasure of finally living the life that they both longed for.

~ cccxxiv ~

"You know God is truly amazing," Jasmine says to her husband as they stroll up the stairs to their bedroom to get dressed.

"I know I thank him every day for you and my baby girl. Like they say, he doesn't show up when you want him to, but when he does, he shows out."

Vanessa sits down the street from Jordan's home. She watches as his guest arrive for his New Year's Eve bash that he throws every year. Every day she is reminded of how good she had it when she was with Jordan, but because of her lustfulness, she lost everything. Thomas has even abandoned her and his little girl because his family was threatening to disown him.

Vanessa glances back at her daughter who is sound asleep in the back sit, she feels sorry for her child. "Another child will have to grow up without a dad," she says a loud.

Vanessa continues to sit when she sees Alexis's car pull up.

"What the hell is she doing here? I know Jordan did not invite her stupid ass."

Vanessa watches as Alexis enters the house, "Oh no she didn't. If she can go inside so can I."

Vanessa looks back at her daughter, "I'll be right back sweetheart."

Vanessa gets out of the car and heads of the walkway but before she can get close to the door, she is stopped in her tracks.

Alexis makes her way inside and immediately sees Jordan. She walks over to where he is.

"Alexis, what the hell are you doing here? How dare you show your face in my home?"

"Jordan I need to talk with you about something. I know what type of person you are and I thought since I cooperated with the police to testify against my brother, you would do me a favor."

Jordan laughs.

"You have lost your darn mind if you think I would do anything for you after all the heartache you and your brother caused me. I am the reason you are out of jail right now. So I think I have done all that I need to."

"Jordan please help me, I have no one to turn to."

"Leave my home Alexis," Jordan shouts."

Alexis reaches for the gun that is in her jacket and points it at Jordan's head.

"I did not want this to go down this way, but you leave me with no choice. I want two hundred thousand tonight and I will leave peacefully, if not, your little girl will grow up without a father."

"Alexis, I do not keep that type of cash around the house. I will have to go to the bank when it opens."

"Wrong answer."

Vanessa grows tired of the foolishness with one of Jordan's staff and pushes him out of the way of the door. She enters the house and sees Jordan and Alexis. She makes her way over and stands in front of him just as Alexis pulls the trigger.

The gunshot is heard all through the house. Vanessa falls to the ground as Ronnie and Matthew tackle Alexis to the ground.

Jordan reaches down and holds Vanessa in his arms.

"Vanessa hold on, you are going to be okay. Someone call the paramedics!" Jordan yells.

"My baby!"

"Your baby?" Jordan repeats.

"She is outside in the car," Vanessa speaks her last words in order to save her daughter's life.

About the author

Denise Hill was raised in Indianapolis, Indiana where she still resides with her son Daniel and daughter Devin. She works at one of the largest financial institution in Indianapolis as a Sales and Marketing Associate and has been employed there for over 27 years. Denise graduated from Thomas Carr Howe High School and earned her Business degree from the University of Phoenix. Denise has always enjoyed writing and decided to try her hand at writing her first Romance and Suspense novel. Denise is currently working on other novels and hopes to see this novel on film in the near future.